D1733524

*W*hat the critics are saying...

"Full of dark sensual passion, *Sacred Circle* will entice and enthrall a person into reading this mysterious but intriguing book. ...Grace and Julian are like two lost lovers finding their way back to each other. *Ms. Thompson* has created a story unlike I have ever read before but I know that if this is anything to go by, this author will be one I will read again and again." ~ *Sheryl for eCataRomance Reviews*

"*Sacred Circle* is a wonderful book that grabs the reader's attention. ...Julian is sexy and dark with a definite alpha attitude and sensual personality. ...The sparks fly when Grace meets Julian and the love scenes are hot. Vampire lovers will find this book a must read and a definite keeper." ~ *Angel Brewer for Romance Studio*

"This is *Claire Thompson's* first venture into the world of the vampire, though far from her first book. And this reviewer sincerely hopes it is only the first of more to come! The plot flowed and carried the reader along...to the last page...Julian was the perfect vampire: strong handsome and sure of himself and his powers, and with scruples and capable of great passion. Yet not perfect! This reviewer found the differences to the vampiric ways that

Ms Thompson introduced utterly natural and totally refreshing." ~ *Kitty for Love Romances*

"...*Sacred Circle* is a story of the lengths a person will go to in order to find their true self. It requires going outside the comfort zone to be truly happy and fulfilled. It is also a palatable story of a dominant/submissive relationship for those who are not into hardcore BDSM." ~ *Darnée for Coffee Time Romance*

"...This book is a true blending of souls. I fell in love with both of these tremendous characters. Julian has had the experience of time; while Grace has been fighting something she knew nothing about in herself. The beauty comes from self-discovery and the bonding between the two of these characters. Ms. Thompson has outdone herself with this story." ~ *Laura for Enchanted in Romance*

CLAIRE THOMPSON

SACRED

CIRCLE

ELLORA'S CAVE
ROMANTICA PUBLISHING

An Ellora's Cave Romantica Publication

www.ellorascave.com

Sacred Circle

ISBN # 1419952730
ALL RIGHTS RESERVED.
Sacred Circle Copyright© 2005 Claire Thompson
Edited by Mary Moran
Cover art by Christine Clavel

Electronic book Publication April 2005
Trade paperback Publication October 2005

Excerpt from *Turning Tricks* Copyright © Claire Thompson 2005

With the exception of quotes used in reviews, this book may not be reproduced or used in whole or in part by any means existing without written permission from the publisher, Ellora's Cave Publishing, Inc.® 1056 Home Avenue, Akron OH 44310-3502.

This book is a work of fiction and any resemblance to persons, living or dead, or places, events or locales is purely coincidental. The characters are productions of the authors' imagination and used fictitiously.

Warning:

The following material contains graphic sexual content meant for mature readers. *Sacred Circle* has been rated *E-rotic* by a minimum of three independent reviewers.

Ellora's Cave Publishing offers three levels of Romantica™ reading entertainment: S (S-ensuous), E (E-rotic), and X (X-treme).

S-*ensuous* love scenes are explicit and leave nothing to the imagination.

E-*rotic* love scenes are explicit, leave nothing to the imagination, and are high in volume per the overall word count. In addition, some E-rated titles might contain fantasy material that some readers find objectionable, such as bondage, submission, same sex encounters, forced seductions, etc. E-rated titles are the most graphic titles we carry; it is common, for instance, for an author to use words such as "fucking", "cock", "pussy", etc., within their work of literature.

X-*treme* titles differ from E-rated titles only in plot premise and storyline execution. Unlike E-rated titles, stories designated with the letter X tend to contain controversial subject matter not for the faint of heart.

Also by Claire Thompson:

Sacred Circle

To my editor and friend, Mary Moran, who gives me inspiration, gentle guidance and honest criticism.

Chapter One

He'd sensed something, a presence, but now it was gone. There was another like him among the throng. Julian looked quickly around the large hall, taking in the crowds of people, most dressed in black, talking and laughing in groups or clustered around the bar. He'd "crashed" the party, after seeing the signs in the lobby for the *Vampire Coven Ball – By Invitation Only*. These events occasionally amused him, and it had been easy to slip by the two hulking fellows at the door, diligently checking people's invitations before allowing access to the grand ballroom of this fine, old Garden District hotel.

Julian hadn't been to New Orleans in longer than he could recall. He had almost forgotten the lush, hothouse atmosphere of the city in summertime. New Orleans barely seemed like it belonged in the States—reminding him more of a European town, except for the interminable muggy heat! Why did anyone build a city here at all, below sea level in a malarial swamp infested with snakes and alligators?

He well remembered those early days, when the adventurous and the criminal converged in their efforts to control the Mississippi River and to trade on it. At first, the town grew topsy-turvy. By 1840, it was the fourth biggest city in the States. In its humid, fever-ridden isolation, it was also by some margin the most exotic. With its mix of Creole, Cajun, Caribbean, African, Irish, Italian, German,

Jewish and everyone else Julian could think of, it had mutated into something unique in the world.

And so it remained today, in a new millennium. The sparkling new buildings and showcase museums couldn't alter the basic sultry character so unique to the Big Easy. Julian still preferred wandering the cobblestone streets of the French Quarter, which harkened back to his own roots in France, so long ago.

Julian stood tall, easily six-foot. This was nothing remarkable in this day and age, but when Julian had been born, over three hundred years ago, such height was rare. His hair was black, falling in soft waves, curling just below his ears. His face was long and sensitively shaped, the cheekbones prominent, the chin strong. His eyes were large and dark against his pale skin, and fringed with thick lashes that made him seem innocent.

Julian was far from innocent. Nor was he young. Unlike the players and pretenders at this party, Julian was, in fact, the real thing. There weren't so many left in the world today — perhaps only ten thousand.

Despite the popular belief that vampires are immortal, in fact they do die, as do all things on this earth. Though it is true, the aging process is dramatically slowed once a vampire reaches maturity. Julian, at the chronological age of three hundred and twelve, looked like a man of perhaps thirty years.

He had been "turned" by a vampire those many years ago, when he was only twenty years old. He would never forget Adrienne. Technically speaking she wasn't his first lover — he'd had several quick tumbles in the hay with willing girls who knew as little as he of the ways of the flesh. But Adrienne was the first one to involve his heart and mind. She had been older than he, how much older he had had no idea at the time, thinking her simply a worldly lady from Paris, come to his father's lands in the Provinces.

La Comtesse Adrienne de Pierre Rouchard, despite her lofty title and incredible wealth, appeared as a young woman, perhaps only in her late twenties. Julian's father Andre, widowed many years before, was known to receive the occasional nobility at his extensive vineyards in the Champagne region. His fine wines were sought after all over France and beyond, their restrained richness created from a perfect blend of the best grapes. Though he himself was not of noble lineage, Andre was educated, sophisticated and always ready with an abundant table and wine cellar when his guests came to call.

La Comtesse, having met Andre Gaston in Paris, accepted his gracious invitation to visit his estate, arriving with a small entourage one spring evening, prepared to stay for several days.

Julian recalled the first time he'd set eyes upon her. Her hair had been darkest black, elaborately arranged on her head in the style of the day, with little gleaming jewels artfully braided through it. Her skin was pale, but not sallow. There was a peculiar, almost luminous quality to her skin, a quality he would later come to recognize as a mark of a vampire, and a quality he would come to share. Her lips were painted a ruby red, exactly the shade of the jewels in her hair.

When she laughed, and she laughed often, Julian noted her small, white, even teeth. He noted the little canines, which seemed slightly longer than the other teeth, but not so much that one would think much about it. Her eyes were dark, and though small, seemed to sparkle with some kind of secret, especially when she turned them upon young Julian.

He had been placed next to her on the first evening that she dined with the family. The long dining table was lavishly set and almost sagging with food, fine china and bottles of Andre's hearty wines and delicate champagnes. Clustered around the long oval table, in addition to Julian and to his father seated grandly at the head of the table, were Julian's six brothers and sisters, a maiden aunt and several important luminaries from the nearby village who wouldn't have missed viewing La Comtesse for the world.

Adrienne had chatted gaily with the men, offering her opinions on every subject. Julian's sisters and aunts, who had been taught from an early age to keep their thoughts and opinions to themselves unless specifically asked, listened with widening eyes as the learned woman gave her views on everything from the quality of the grape harvest that year to the politics of the day, and even the French monarchy. Andre and the other men seemed enchanted, and as many bottles of fine wine were consumed, began to loudly toast her, their glasses clinking, their laughter loud, their faces red.

Yet, it was Julian to whom Adrienne continually turned, quietly asking his opinion on any number of subjects, and seeming fascinated as he tried to stammer out his responses. Ah, Adrienne—she was a master at making a young man feel bold and wise. Julian recalled his own feelings of pride and confidence as she bolstered him with assurances and unfailing interest in his no doubt stupid comments.

Her hand slipped softly to his hard-muscled thigh and Julian started, feeling heat creep up his cheeks. She did not meet his eye, yet there was no question that she knew her hand was where it didn't belong. Her long slender fingers moved slowly up his leg, causing the young man to blush. He hid his confusion and arousal with a long drink of his wine. She stopped just short of his cock, which was now fully erect and straining painfully against his breaches.

Julian recalled his own embarrassment on that long ago evening, mixed with a raging desire. How he longed for those perfect fingers to touch his cock, and yet he knew if she had touched him there, he would have ejaculated on the spot, in front of his entire family and died a thousand deaths of humiliation. Adrienne, though, knew just how far to tease, and she withdrew her hand, still never having met his eye, still holding a lively discourse.

Finally, the festivities wound down, and Adrienne excused herself, pleading exhaustion. Julian was also tired, though still wildly aroused by the countess' secret attentions. Alone in his room as he stripped off his clothing, his cock again rose of its own accord, the image of her white, ample breasts pressed alluringly together in the front of his thoughts, the imprint of her soft hand still hot upon his thigh.

"Julian." He'd heard a whisper at his door, which was opened a crack. At first, he thought it was his little sister Louise.

Already in his bed and completely naked, Julian responded, "Go away. I'm sleeping." His own hand gripped his large cock—ready to take what pleasure he could there in the dark.

He heard a soft, low chuckle and realized with a start this was not his sister. The door opened, and Adrienne slipped in silently. She was dressed in white lace, her breasts now free of their boned corset and heavily stayed bodice. Her hair was loose, streaming past her shoulders like a dark waterfall. Against the backdrop of a setting moon, she looked like nothing so much as an angel, fallen from the heavens.

Julian gasped. He'd never had a woman in his rooms, never dared. "Comtesse!" he said, dumbfounded.

"Julian, please call me Adrienne." She moved swiftly toward him, speaking in a low, seductive voice. "Don't worry, my love. No one saw me come in. I can be very discreet when I so choose. I have a gift that way." She smiled enigmatically.

Julian was conflicted. His father would not be pleased to find a woman in Julian's chambers, and he suspected Andre would be especially possessive of this particular woman. Julian started to protest, "My father—"

"Is sleeping soundly, I assure you." Adrienne was at his bedside now, kneeling next to him. Something in her tone calmed Julian. He wanted to believe that it was safe to have her here, but even if it wasn't, he wouldn't have cared. She was too beautiful, and his good fortune seemed boundless now that she was in the room. Let him pay the price later. He must have her.

Ah, and what a price he'd paid. Would he have had it any other way, knowing now that she was going to end his mortal life that night? When she had seduced him, he'd found an ecstasy he had never dreamed of, as her long pale fingers unlocked the sensual secrets of lovemaking for him.

She'd dropped the lacey garments, revealing her rounded, supple body in its perfection. Her breasts were full and lush, the tips glistening in the moonlight. She actually lifted them with her hands, offering herself to

Julian. He didn't need a second invitation, but fell upon her, sucking like a greedy babe.

She laughed, a low sensuous sound, but Julian could barely hear her over the roaring of his own blood. When she climbed over him, just the touch of her satin thighs against his bare penis sent an explosion of pleasure coursing through him, and he spurted his seed against her. "Such a boy," she crooned, laughing still. Julian blushed, ashamed of his overeager body, but Adrienne only shook her head, smiling and laid a finger on his lips.

"Hush, then, my love. To me, this is only a testament of your desire. A high compliment indeed, from such a strong and beautiful lover." Even his premature ejaculation had been made to seem like something sexy and powerful. Julian felt his blood burn hot as her cool fingers took his member, massaging him skillfully so that within moments he was again erect.

Perhaps it was his own shame at having behaved like a boy or his own natural dominant impulses, which had so far only been tested with his farm-girl lovers. Whatever the reason, Julian felt his passion rising on a tide of vengeful lust. Who was this woman, who came to his bed unbidden and had her way with him? He was a man and she a mere woman! Flipping her easily off him, he loomed up, his strong, young form hard and taut over her supple, impossible perfection. He stared down at her alabaster beauty, at the full, rounded breasts with pale-tipped nipples jutting toward him like an offering, at the smooth curve of her rounded belly. Adrienne laid still, her mouth hiding a barely suppressed smile that only egged Julian on. Roughly his lips met hers, tearing a kiss from her as he pulled her body up to his, feeling her firm, large breasts mash against his chest. Desire seared through him like a flame.

Adrienne responded to his kiss, her tongue seeking his as she murmured and moaned against his mouth. He let her go, dropping her back down to the bed as he rose over her again, prepared this time to take her like a man. But something in her face, in her fingers reaching up to smooth his cheek gave him pause. Somehow, she silently commanded him to lie back and he obeyed, barely aware of what was happening, only that he must have her.

Keeping her eyes upon his, Adrienne lifted herself over him and lowered her body until he felt the wet heat of her sex against the tip of his cock. He moaned, and she leaned over, her dark hair dragging across his chest. She opened her mouth, and he opened his, expecting a kiss. Her perfect little teeth suddenly seemed pointed, at least the two canines, but surely it was a trick of the moonlight. Slowly she bent to kiss him, her tongue teasing. She bit down, gently at first, then harder, against his full lower lip. He felt a prick of pain and tasted his own blood. Just as quickly, the pain was eased as she suckled gently against his mouth.

Julian moaned with pleasure as Adrienne lowered herself completely onto his penis, her strong hands pressing against his bare chest for balance. She sat up straight—her head back so that her white throat gleamed in the silvery light. Julian licked his lips, his tongue nursing the spot that had been punctured. As Adrienne leaned forward, Julian saw her parted lips, the little sharp teeth white against them. She smiled lazily at him, and there was power in that smile as she ground her hips against his pelvis. Julian realized he couldn't take his eyes from hers, even if he'd wanted to.

Had he been horrified or at least surprised when he'd realized she had bitten his lip, and then sucked the blood while she rode his cock? He couldn't remember now. All he could recall was that he himself felt blind and dumb with lust. She could have done anything to him, as long as she kept her tight delicious cunt wrapped around his hard cock.

She had spread her legs, pulling him into her hot, tight center. At the moment of climax, he again felt the stinging prick of her kiss, this time at his throat though it barely registered as his pleasure exploded into her.

As his orgasm receded, he became aware that the woman was still locked in a peculiar embrace at his neck. Now he felt the pain, sharp as needles against his throat, as she sucked greedily at his life's blood. His heart pounded as he gasped for air. He felt the pulse where she sucked gently throbbing in rhythm to her tugging mouth.

Julian tried to pull away from her, but she was powerful—far more so than he, though he himself was strong and at the peak of manhood.

Don't struggle, she whispered in his head. *Surrender to me, beautiful boy.* Her mouth remained locked onto his pulse, her face obscured. But he had heard her words, as clearly as if she had spoken aloud. She continued, her voice like a clear bell inside his head. *I have chosen you, Julian. You are to become one with me now. I am taking your life, but I will return it to you, a thousand-fold. Surrender. Give yourself to me. You will never regret it.*

He had no choice. He was ensconced in her embrace, his beating heart thrumming between them. The beating slowed, and slowed again, until his eyes fluttered shut and he felt as if he were leaving his body. He was being lifted, held in her warm, safe embrace. He found that his penis was again erect, and that she was gently easing it back into the hot sweetness of her sex.

Yes, she whispered in his fevered brain, her mouth still suckling at his weakened pulse. Finally, she released his neck, and his head fell back. He was in a swoon, a kind of trance, only dimly aware of what was happening. He tried to ask her, to speak, but his lips wouldn't comply, his mind wouldn't obey.

Adrienne cradled her lover with one hand, pulling him deeper into herself. With her other hand, she unscrewed the little cap of a very small two-handled glass bottle that she wore at her throat on a golden chain. Its lip was sharp, and she drew it now across her wrist, expertly opening a vein hidden beneath her pale, firm skin. Slowly, her eyes locked on Julian, she licked the cut.

Julian was dimly aware that she'd cut herself, that she was going to bleed to death. But instead of a gush of blood, little droplets beaded up in neat little rows, like a perfect offering. As the sweet, red puddle of bright blood bubbled up against her white flesh, she lifted her wrist to Julian's parted lips, daubing them with the sweet nectar. Julian's eyes opened wide as the blood trickled into his mouth.

It was only later that he learned of the properties of vampire saliva. The special ingredients which act as coagulants and anticoagulants, controlling the flow of blood until the vampire has taken his fill, then instantly sealing the wound. Thus could she offer herself in a way dangerous to humans, but safe when managed by a skilled vampire such as Adrienne.

The taste of her blood was indescribable. It was, quite simply, the most lovely and perfect thing to ever have passed his lips. Nothing before or since could compare, though he had traveled the world many times over in search of that elixir.

But for that moment, he drank his fill, sucking at her wrist like a starving babe while she held him in the velvet embrace of her sex, rocking and soothing him. Julian felt himself changing there in her arms. If it was bizarre to be sucking the blood from a lover, the lover who had just pierced his throat and stolen his life's blood, then so be it.

Nothing had ever felt more right, and Julian actually cried when Adrienne finally pulled away from him, denying him another suckle—oh, just one more kiss! *Sleep now, my love*, she whispered, still not moving her lips. He heard her plainly and answered, "Yes," before falling into a dreamless, fevered sleep that would last for three days.

* * * * *

When he awoke, his family had been hovering anxiously about him, but La Comtesse Adrienne had vanished. Julian's first words upon awakening were for her. He felt a slow pulse of need, as if she had replaced his very blood with her own essence. When he was finally coherent enough to ask for her, Andre told him she had left two days before, on some urgent business.

Julian was bereft, inconsolable. It was beyond mere passion, beyond first love. Without understanding why, he craved her as a submissive dog longs for its master. He fingered the two little marks at his neck, now almost healed. He remembered the sweet taste of her blood. Of her blood! Ah, for some blood. Instinctively he knew that only human blood would do. *The soul is lodged in the blood*—these words came unbidden into his mind. Blood—the source of life. He knew that his own life now depended on the blood of the living. What was he to do with this knowledge? What had she done to him?

Julian sensed that he mustn't share these peculiar thoughts of bloodlust with his family. Instead, he focused on the woman, demanding from his father where she had gone, and how to contact her. His father was at first indulgent, assuming his oldest son was suffering from puppy love, but grew angry when Julian refused to let the matter drop. "That fever has addled your mind, boy! I admit, she's a lovely woman, but be realistic! Why would she, a countess of wealth and power, stoop to an affair with a country boy?"

Julian bit back his retort. He desperately wanted to confess that not only had she stooped, but she'd conquered, and now she was all he could think of. Julian realized he would have no allies among his father's household in his efforts to find Adrienne and somehow win her back. He vowed to himself that he would find her. Against his father's wishes, he packed his things, embarking on a journey that would take him all over the world a dozen times or more.

Chapter Two

She had left him a letter, which he still kept in his possession. He had had it recopied and then laminated, as the original paper had disintegrated. He recalled the words now, which had long ago been committed to his heart.

23 May 1712

My Dearest Julian,

I have committed a crime, and I will pay for that crime. Yet, I am not sorry, even now, as I flee from you, and from the Elders of my Circle, who will surely kill me when they find what I have done. Julian, though you now only have a glimmer of what it means, I am a vampire.

I know you cannot possibly understand what has happened to you, but in a moment of weakness, I have taken your pathetic human existence, and bestowed upon you a vampire's life. We vampires are not immortals, as your folklore may have persuaded you. But we do have the gift of extended life, greatly extended. I myself have seen many decades and hope to see many more. Your father and his entire entourage will become nothing but a dim memory of a time that once was. But you, my love, you will continue – I have given you the gift of the sacred kin!

Yet, what I have done is a crime. It was truly a crime of passion, my love. It was as if I were possessed. It was not merely your perfect young body, far from it. I have had my fill of beautiful young men, I can assure you. But there is something different about you, my Julian. Something special. I sensed the mark of greatness upon you, and I was overcome with longing.

Your spirit is so strong and beautiful! Oh, to think I shall never see you again! Because I must not. They will be tracking you now, in hopes of finding me. They most likely already know what I have done, as we in my Circle are psychically linked.

You now have the power. I have turned you, Julian. It is forbidden to turn a human into a vampire, without consent from the Elders, and without a clear understanding on the part of the human involved as to what will occur. This turning is rare now. Indeed many vampires, unlike myself, tend to keep their distance from humans, only coming out at night to take the weak. I never fully understood this hesitation before now, for I never felt the overwhelming temptation to turn a human as I did with you. I didn't prepare you. You had no warning and no say in the matter.

It was my own weakness, which led me astray. I could have killed you, my love. I should have. There are no vampiric laws against killing humans. You are such fragile beings, and so easily disposed of. There are so many of you, what is one more or less?

Yet, I dislike the casual killing of humans. I have become very fond of some. Your father was among them, though now I must never visit him again. Other vampires call me sentimental, and I suppose I am. They will slake their blood-thirst by sucking out the life of a human, then tossing its husk aside with barely a thought.

And yet, we are forbidden to "create". Only the Elders decide, and this code is inviolate. Hence, I must flee, my love. We shared but one night. I hadn't meant to turn you. I only planned to make love to that perfect body.

You can perhaps blame yourself, my love, for it was your perfection that turned a woman's heart, and cost her her judgment and now her freedom. I am doomed, from that one kiss, to spend the rest of my days hiding, in secret, never again to see those of my Circle. An outcast.

I know I shall come to regret it, but for now, with the sweet taste of your blood still on my lips, and the lovely, ragged pain of the cut at my wrist, I regret nothing. Perhaps one day things will change, and we will be reunited. But for now, my young lover, my Julian, we must part.

The Elders will find you when it is time, and you will learn all you need to know. Though rigid in their edicts, they are also fair, and they will not leave you to wander the earth without guidance or understanding.

I must fly, as the hour when the dawn turns the mountains golden is at hand.

Take care!

Forgive me. Adrienne

Julian sighed a little as he recalled her words, written so long ago yet still with the power to wrench his heart. The pulsing rhythms of the modern music around him brought him back to the present day. He was standing very still against a wall in the crowded ballroom. Normal humans wouldn't notice him there unless he moved. He had the vampire's art of becoming almost invisible at will, blending into the shadows like a half-forgotten dream.

Silently, he surveyed the room, searching with his psychic powers for the presence he had felt a moment before. Perhaps he had imagined it. It was rare to encounter another of his kind these days, especially in this country. Though, if he were going to, it would probably be here in New Orleans. He felt lonely for a moment, something he rarely allowed himself the luxury of feeling. For what was the point?

He liked humans but they aged so quickly. He rarely became attached, as he hated to watch them wither and die, while he himself barely seemed to change from year to year, century to century.

The first hundred years or so after he had been turned had been exciting. Instead of hating Adrienne for what she had done, he had been thrilled. To be forever young! His strength, already formidable as a mere human, had increased fourfold at least. His powers of perception, of sight, sound and smell were heightened, giving him the advantage over mere mortals.

The Elders did find him. Two stately men contacted him. He came to know them as Gustav and Augustine. They sent a message, inviting him to a local tavern. Unlike Adrienne, still full of vitality and bursting with sensuality, these two men were staid. Their skin still had the luminous quality he would come to associate with his own kind, but it was thin, almost papery. It was clear they were very old and yet, their faces were smooth, their eyes keen. That was what had confused him, he realized. He'd been expecting the sagging, wrinkled skin of someone ancient. Vampires, he came to learn, aged differently.

"Adrienne has committed a crime," Gustav told him solemnly. "When we find her, she will die." Gustav went on to outline the nature of her crime, and why she must pay with her life. Julian had tried to focus on their words, but that threat was all he could hear. His beloved Adrienne, who had given him this new life, was to die.

"It is not your fault that you've been turned," Augustine said. "We will take you into our Circle and teach you our ways. Though it was without your consent or understanding, you are now one of us. One of the true kin. We are a solitary people, but the Dark Circle, our coven, will always be there for you now."

Julian spent many days with these Elders, learning secrets shared only among their kind. When they parted, Julian had a large leather pouch filled with gold sovereigns and precious jewels. He was also given papers that would gain him access to the larger European banks, and an account that would satisfy his needs as long as he roamed the world. "One thing we have is time," Gustav had explained. "We have investments that date back centuries. Our combined wealth is unparalleled in the human world. Even we vampires need homes, lodging, clothing. As you are now part of our Circle, you will never want, at least financially."

Finally, Julian parted from the Elders, beginning his quest for his first love. The Elders had tried to advise him on the safest ways to use humans without undue harm. Their interest was less in sparing human lives, which neither of them seemed to hold in very high regard, but more in how to avoid drawing attention to oneself. It wouldn't do to have people suddenly dying from loss of blood whenever you appeared in town. It was admittedly difficult to avoid. Humans were, after all, such fragile beings. Thus, they advised him never to stay anywhere too long as eventually suspicions would invariably turn toward him.

The memory of his first killing was still fresh even now, almost three hundred years later. It would be some time before he learned to quench his thirst without taking a human life. Each time he did, he swore it would be the last. But the bloodlust came upon him like a fever. During those times, his finer senses were forgotten as he focused on his next victim.

It was dusk, and Julian had only ridden a few hundred leagues from his father's lands. A farmer was cutting his grain when Julian came upon him. He'd accidentally cut himself rather badly with his scythe and was sitting in the middle of the field, holding his shoulder.

Julian, riding on the path nearby first smelled the blood, his senses pricking up sharply at the pungent glorious scent. Veering his horse to track it, he came upon the hapless man, bright red blood spurting between his fingers. The man's face was gray with pain.

Leaping from his steed, Julian knelt to help him. Though he'd never been attracted to another man before, Julian was no longer the man he had been. The smell of blood filled his nostrils like something tangible. He breathed it, sighing deeply, and his penis engorged and distended of its own accord.

It wasn't the man himself that aroused Julian, but the promise of blood, beckoning like a lover. At first, he tried to help the man, tearing a piece of his own clothing to staunch the flow. Tying off the cloth tourniquet, he saw that the bleeding was actually slowing. Blood had soaked the man's pants and the ground beside him. It became clear that the cut was too deep and the man was dying.

Abandoning any efforts to save him, Julian instead seized his chance. He must drink before life fled. The Elders had taught him that the human prey must be alive for the blood to quench his vampire's thirst. Sitting down on the hard dirt, Julian took the poor farmer onto his lap, cradling him like a child. He was insensible now and made no protest.

The white linen that tied off the wound was red-soaked, but Julian wasn't interested in the wound itself. He wanted the throat, he realized. The delicate jugular. Leaning down, he bit, piercing the flesh, which yielded like butter to his kiss. He felt the blood fill him like liquid fire. It gushed against his teeth, filling his mouth so that he had to swallow quickly to keep from choking. Later he would learn to moderate the flow, making the kiss last for hours at a time if so desired.

But now, he sucked greedily, feeling his sexual lust rise as his blood-thirst was slaked. When at last Julian released the man, he fell back lifeless, his pulse gone, his eyes open to the darkening sky.

Julian pushed the dead man from his lap. After closing the unseeing eyes, Julian stripped, balling his bloodied clothing and stuffing it into a saddlebag before retrieving new. He mounted his patiently waiting horse and went in search of a wench to satisfy his other hunger.

Her name was Vivien. A sweet little lass, though not innocent in ways of the flesh. When he'd arrived at the nearest town, he found an inn that could lodge his horse and give him a room for the night. When the serving girl came to his door with fresh bedding, Julian eyed her soft bosom. Her cleavage was deep above the simple cotton gown she wore. Unlike the noblewomen and landed gentry, peasants couldn't afford the fancy corsets and bodices that would hide and restrain a woman's natural offering.

Julian, still fiercely aroused from his first human blood, felt the fire burning in his veins. He leaned down, boldly drawing his finger across one supple breast. "Well, sir!" Vivien said, feigning horrified surprise. In fact, Julian, handsome even before the change, was subtly altered by Adrienne's gift.

His large dark eyes now sparkled with a fire that made whatever woman he chose sigh and open herself to him without reservation. His dark shiny hair curled seductively over his fine, high forehead and around the back of his strong neck. His mouth had a new sensuality, a hint of cruelty blended into a smile that had lost its innocence when he lost his human life.

Bending toward her, he whispered, "Tell me your name, pretty girl."

"Vivien," she whispered breathlessly. Reaching around her small waist, Julian drew her into the room.

"Please, sir," she had protested weakly, "I must go. My father is waiting."

"No, you will stay. I will explain to your father that you are detained." He dropped his mouth to hers, kissing her with a passion fueled by the powerful bloodlust still coursing through his veins.

Again she tried to protest, but her words were muffled by his mouth on hers. Not realizing his own newly made strength, his attempt to open her gown resulted in his tearing it from her body. Vivien was completely naked underneath. She screamed, trying to pull away from him.

He could feel her heart beating against him as he held her warm naked body to him. Covering her mouth with his hand, he whispered in her ear, "Quiet, quiet, silly girl. I must have you. You are so lovely. Don't worry, I'll replace the dress with three new ones. Don't resist me. Hush." He pulled her head back so that he could see her face. She turned her frightened eyes toward his, her mouth still covered by his strong hand.

All at once she relaxed, her eyes still locked on his. It was his first brush with the knowledge of his power over humans. He could control them with his eyes and bend them to his will.

More slowly came the psychic powers, the ability to enter another's mind. At first, he could only distinguish feelings — the fear, the rage, the desire of those he "chose". But slowly, with much concentration, he learned to untangle the jumble of psychic chatter and random emotion, distinguishing thoughts and learning to separate them from feelings.

With Vivien, he was still new and untested. He could sense her fear mingled with a rising desire. Effortlessly he lifted her, dropping her onto the large feather bed in the middle of the room. Her ample breasts were heaving and her mouth gaped open as she tried to draw a shuddering breath.

Julian dropped his hands to her legs, forcing them apart. He pressed a finger into her entrance, feeling it slick and wet, despite her fear or perhaps partially because of it. He sensed her arousal. She wanted to be taken — to be raped!

Julian's lust was fueled by the fact that he was taking her by force. A gentle man before the change, he found himself emboldened by his lust. With a primal growl, he pulled his own shirt from his strongly muscled torso. Unbuttoning his leather breeches, he kicked off his boots at the same time.

Vivien's eyes dropped to his erection, rock-hard and perpendicular to his flat stomach. "Do you want it, wench?" he demanded, his voice husky with lust. "Do you want this big, strong man to take his pleasure, to use you like a common whore?" He didn't wait for her answer, didn't care what she had to say. The words incited him further, as he hoisted himself over her.

No tender kisses, no murmured sweetness. Guiding his large cock with his hand, he found her entrance, still wet but tight, and pressed into her. Vivien squealed, trying to close her legs. "I'm going to take you, wench, so you can either lie back and enjoy it or suffer. It makes no difference to me."

In fact, it did make a difference. He realized as he spoke that it was her fear, more than her desire or her beauty that excited him. Her squeals of terror and pain as he forced his cock into her made him as hard as iron. "Take it!" he cried, as he thrust himself deep inside of her. He felt his own power like a drug. He would travel the world, taking what he wanted, feeding his own bloodlust and his sexual appetites. Vivien was the first of many who would fall prey to his passions.

As he moved his hips, savoring the hot, tight clamp of her sex against him, he became aware that she was no longer struggling. Her eyes were closed and when he removed his hand from her mouth, the only sound was of her labored breathing and breathy little sighs. Julian felt her passion rising to meet his. At that moment, it was perfect, just what he needed to send him over the sweet edge of sexual release.

He had left her there, sleeping on the bed she had come to prepare, a little smile on her lips, a gold sovereign pressed into her limp hand.

Chapter Three

The blood-hunger was both a psychological and physical sensation. It wasn't satisfied by food or drink, but only by human blood. It would start as a whispered gnawing in his gut, but eventually it would overtake him. While in the throes of this need, he was at once agitated and empowered. His pulse would race, and he would feel a dizzying fever overcome him in anticipation of the act of feeding.

Eventually, Julian finally learned to control his baser instincts. He learned to survive on less and to take the blood of humans without killing them. His passion for blood raged as much as ever, but he was able to spare the lives of his victims, for the most part.

He was careful never to mix sex and bloodlust, as he knew he might not be able to exercise the control necessary to spare the life of his lover. And, remembering his dear Adrienne, lost forever to him, he had never attempted to "turn" a human, as she had so rashly done with him. Indeed, the Elders had told him many years after the turning that they were surprised he had survived.

Turning was a special skill and very few vampires could accomplish it. Humans were simply too fragile as a rule, and the offering was lost when they gave up their flimsy lives, overpowered by the vampire's rich and perfect blood. Vampires were a dying breed as less and less of them retained the art of turning, and slowly, finally, the ancient ones died away at last. Procreation was rare and required special circumstances. The birth of a new vampire was heralded across the globe. It had been years since Julian had heard of such a thing. He himself, though he'd lain with vampires, had never created life.

Julian shook his head, trying to focus in the present. The music, some kind of techno beat, pulsed around him. He moved a little from the wall, all his senses alert. Walking slowly, he raked his eyes over the throng of people. Most of them looked as though they were at a costume party, with the theme being Count Dracula, of course. He was vaguely amused by these silly humans, but he also knew there were some serious players among them. People who honestly believed they themselves were vampires.

At first, Julian had been interested by the rise in the twentieth and twenty-first centuries of these so-called vampire clubs. He'd been fascinated by the plethora of them springing up on the Internet, and the profusion of information that flooded the web about "real vampires". Most of it was utter nonsense but some of it was right on the money. As always, there was a kernel of truth in the mass of misinformation.

He had penetrated a few of the vampire clubs, only to learn that the people involved were mostly players, using blood and blood-play as a way to feel special, or to enhance kinky BDSM sex games.

Some of the humans in the groups seemed convinced of their own authenticity. They professed a sensitivity to light and a need for human blood to survive. At first, Julian used to try to explain that drinking blood didn't make you a vampire — it made you a person with a blood-fetish. Too few of them could distinguish the difference. Eventually his earnest attempts to educate gave way to tolerant amusement. Let them play their games. What was the harm in it?

Usually he avoided these vampire playgroups, because they depressed him, reminding him of how alone he in fact was. There were only a handful of his own circle now left, and they were presently scattered over the globe. He had given up any hope of finding Adrienne. She was little more than a passing dream to him now.

He scanned the room. The connection he'd felt a moment before was gone. Perhaps it had only been his longing that twisted its way into his brain, creating the illusion that there was someone here like himself, one of the true kin.

Moving forward, he revealed himself now to the crowd and as always, he was immediately noticed. Handsome as a human, he was triply so now, with his alabaster skin, his dark eyes and his hair dark as a crow's wing. His body was hard and muscular, without a trace of fat and he dressed impeccably in fine linens, leathers and silks.

Several people approached him now, glasses upraised. He turned to meet them, swallowing the sigh of loneliness, his face cast in a red-lipped smile, which didn't reach his eyes.

* * * * *

Grace felt the hairs on the back of her neck rise. There was a delicious smell teasing her senses, but she couldn't quite place it. Something hinting of sage and lemon balm. The scent was something primal, something sexual. Her nipples rose and she felt a warmth in her sex that confused her. When she turned, she could see no one. No one special, that is.

Just the crowd of vampire lifestylers, decked out in their black and crimson cloaks, sporting their store-bought fangs and blood-red lipstick, painted onto faces made pale with powder.

She shifted in her seat, sipping at the Bloody Mary, which was heavily laced with vodka. She must be drunk, she decided. She must be horny, that was all. She would have to scope out the scene, and try to find the good-looking guys, if there were any.

It was her first time at a Vampire Coven Ball and she wasn't exactly sure what she was doing there. Regan had convinced her to come along, because of Grace's longtime interest in vampires. Regan was a role-player, mostly online, and this party had been put together by some of the more serious "players", many of whom were meeting for the first time in the flesh tonight.

Regan had dumped Grace at the bar and gone off with a man named Cloven. Or at least that's what he called himself. Apparently, Regan and Cloven were hot and heavy in their role-play, with Cloven a self-styled "donor", one who gives blood willingly to a "vampire". Of course, none of it was real. It was all an elaborate, if wonderful, game.

Regan spent every spare moment on her computer, when she wasn't working at the law office where both she and Grace were paralegals. She'd tried to involve Grace in the online games but Grace had found them childish, though she hadn't admitted that to Regan, pretending instead that she had no aptitude for it.

Looking around now, Grace found herself feeling dizzy. Was it the Bloody Mary? For the first time in years, thoughts and images she'd banished from her conscious mind came flooding back with a force that staggered her.

That smell again! It was so sweet, so powerful, almost as if something, or someone, were calling her name. *A soul mate. Someone like me. One who shares the bloodlust.* These words burned into her consciousness, startling her so that she gasped aloud. Ridiculous!

The secrets she'd held so close to her heart for these many years came unbidden, bursting into flame in her mind. From the first time when she was fourteen and had tasted her own blood, something had clicked inside of her. Some primal appetite had been awoken. And now at age twenty-four, that appetite raged secretly and unchecked, though largely ignored by its mistress.

At fourteen, she had fallen from her bike, hitting the pavement with her chin. The resulting mouthful of blood had terrified her. Swallowing, she'd inadvertently gulped her own blood, tasting its metallic sweetness with something like shock.

Shock because the constant gnawing that was always in her gut, had been there since the onset of puberty, was suddenly allayed. Though she'd been in pain from the fall, with her mouth cut and bleeding, the blood was like a life force exploding through her veins.

She'd known it from that moment—known that she was "different". She'd also known better than to confide in anyone about her newfound bloodlust. Her mouth had healed, but her passion had been awoken, and it was almost a sexual thing. She craved blood. Animal blood wouldn't do, though usually it was all she had.

She'd once tried purchasing a small bucket of cow's blood from the local slaughterhouse, but it had nauseated her. The stench of offal had permeated the blood, and its dark coagulated offering was sour and foul in her mouth.

No, it had to be human. And where did one find human blood?

She learned a lesson in caution at age fifteen, when she and a best girlfriend made a "blood-pact" to be best friends forever. It had been Grace's idea, though she hadn't consciously admitted her own designs. They'd pricked their index fingers, pressing them together as a way to mingle their "life's blood" as a symbol of eternal friendship.

The sight of that bright, perfect offering had been too much for the young Grace and impulsively she'd grabbed her friend's hand, sucking against the bleeding finger like a starving baby suckling its mother's milk.

Her friend had been upset, pulling back her hand. "Gross! You are really weird, you know that, Grace?" Grace had been startled by her own action and immediately ashamed. Beyond the girl's words, Grace actually *felt* her friend's disgust resonating within her. She could sense the girl's recoiling as a palpable thing. She'd turned away, exerting all of her own willpower to keep from grabbing the girl's hand again, to finish licking a single drop still swaying from its tip.

She'd lost the friend, but learned a lesson in discretion.

Instead of trying to find human blood from others, Grace had become a "cutter", using a razor knife to satisfy her thirst. The little stolen mouthfuls of her own blood allayed the worst of the chronic ache in her gut. Her parents had been alarmed by the little cuts along her arms and inner thighs, and she had been forced to be very careful, only cutting where they wouldn't see.

They worried that she was maladjusted. She'd been "found" as a baby and these parents were the only ones she knew. Now she overheard them clucking with fear that some genetic trait was now manifesting itself and they were in for trouble.

When they'd taken her to a psychiatrist, the offered therapy made her doubt, and finally deny, her true feelings. Her secret longing for blood was dismissed as misplaced fantasy. The therapist convinced her that the cutting was simply a manifestation of her own insecurities, due to the adoption and the onset of puberty. He worked with her to resolve any lingering issues of poor self-esteem and feelings of worthlessness. Because it was easier to accept these explanations, she did.

The heady sweetness of human blood became little more than a dream, the fantasy of an overactive imagination. By age seventeen, she was heavily into denial. She regarded those early feelings of bloodlust as confused adolescent longings. She told herself that she was "cured". And indeed, she did stop cutting herself and she stopped consciously fantasizing about the bright red droplets of life-sustaining energy that had rolled on her tongue like a kiss.

Physically she paid the price, not receiving the nourishment she needed — unaware she was starving herself. Her mother worried her constantly to eat, making thick rich meals that raised Grace's gorge, but obediently she tried to force them down. She learned to hide her constant gnawing pain and the extreme fatigue from her worrying parents, finally accepting it as a part of the fabric of what she was.

Grace desperately wanted to be "normal" in the way of most seventeen-year-old girls who just want to fit in.

She was mostly successful. There was still that ever-present gnawing whisper of hunger in her gut. Food didn't satisfy it, but she learned to ignore it, for the most part.

As she matured, Grace's skin, always fair, became very pale. People often asked her if she were ill, which irritated her. As she learned to use makeup effectively, these questions lessened. Still the quiet pain and fatigue persisted, but Grace became a master of sublimation. She became aware of an increased sensitivity to sunlight. She burned easily in the sun and tended to avoid being outdoors, especially in the summer. No beach vacations or lolling by the pool with friends for Grace.

More likely, she would be found holed up in a library somewhere, reading in a corner, almost hidden by stacks of old books about history and fantasy. While convinced by her therapist and her own desire to be "normal" that there was no such thing as vampires left in the world, Grace still loved to read about the ancient and medieval creatures who rose from the dead, usually during times of plague or great strife, to stalk the world in the dark of night, feeding off humans to slake their constant blood-thirst.

She felt a curious affinity with the dark creatures, fantasizing and yet, if asked, she would laugh and say she just liked the old stories. They were fantastic, that was all. There was nothing to them, of course. They were simply legends trying to explain the unexplainable.

It was during college that Grace discovered the vampire clubs. She'd been accepted to a small liberal arts college in New Orleans and was in the middle of her senior year when she'd met Regan, the Gothic drama queen extraordinaire. Regan dressed exclusively in black and told anyone who would listen that she had been kissed by a real vampire, and had thus been "turned".

Of course, it was understood that Regan was playacting, but just the same, Grace had been intrigued. In her small town in the backwaters of Louisiana, any talk of vampires would have been decried as sacrilegious and even obscene. Grace had been enthralled at the open way Regan had exhibited her taste for blood, and her own professed sensitivity to light. When Regan had offered to exchange a blood-kiss, as she called it, whereby the girls would each prick their thumbs and offer it to the other, Grace had recoiled, the recollection of that other time suddenly emerging from the depths of suppressed memories.

She didn't examine her own reluctance. She didn't have to. A part of her already sensed what was becoming increasingly difficult to deny. Now as she sat at the bar, sipping her tomato juice and vodka, she turned on her stool, seeking the source of the scent that had electrified her. She resisted an impulse to touch her sex and instead crossed her legs, the slight pressure easing a bit of her unexplained arousal.

Looking up, she saw a young man approaching her. He was about her age, perhaps a little older. His face was painted white, with a little droplet of red drawn at the corner of his mouth, which was also painted blood red. His sandy-colored hair was brushed straight back, revealing a strong widow's peak. His look was completed by the requisite black satin cape lined with crimson.

Despite the obvious Count Dracula getup, Grace could see that the guy was rather good-looking, with wide blue eyes and even features, though his jaw was a little weak. He was quite tall and though his shoulders were narrow and a little stooped, still he presented as an attractive man. She noticed a little trinket around his neck, some kind of glass vial.

Perhaps taking this as his cue, the fellow said, "Ah, you are noticing my amulet. Do you like it?" She looked more closely at the little glass bottle. It had a small handle on either side, and tapered at the bottom. It was quite unusual.

"It's quite beautiful. What is it?"

"I can see you are a fledgling," he said with a superior little smile. "You are not an initiate of the covens. My coven is the Red Covenant. No doubt, you've heard of it. Allow me to introduce myself. I am Robert. Robert Dalton. At your service, my lady." As he spoke, Robert bowed low, sweeping his cape around himself with a flourish.

Grace couldn't help but laugh a little at his dramatics. She answered, "I'm Grace. Grace Davis. And I guess I am a fledgling or whatever you called me, because I haven't a clue what you're talking about. Is that your secret decoder ring or something along those lines?" She pointed to his amulet. "And the 'Red Covenant' is your boys' club—no girls allowed?" Of course she knew what a coven was, but it amused her to play dumb at his expense.

Robert smiled back, though the smile now seemed a little strained. Grace could feel his irritation. She seemed to have a knack, a gift her mother said, of actually sensing what others were feeling. Sometimes she almost felt she could hear their thoughts. Usually it made her uncomfortable, like watching someone through the crack in a bathroom stall. She wasn't supposed to be there.

Grace bit her lip. She knew she had insulted him but he was rather pompous, calling her a fledgling—clearly an insult in his book. He lifted his eyebrows and said, "Evidently someone has brought you here, as a *guest*." He almost seemed to spit the word. "I can see you have no knowledge of even the most basic vampire terminology."

Sitting on the empty stool next to Grace, Robert now said, "Allow me to give you a brief lesson. A fledgling is someone who is inexperienced with the vampire lifestyle. New to the scene. Fledglings who are permitted to join a coven are assigned as an apprentice to a more experienced vampire who acts as their mentor, if you will, teaching them about our rituals, duties and sacred codes."

So it is a secret boys' club, she thought, trying to keep an attentive and serious expression as Robert continued. "This talisman that you see indicates my superior status in the Red Covenant. It's called an amphora. Among the ancients, these vessels were used for holding sacred wine or special oils. We sanguine use it for other things." He looked meaningfully at her.

"It's quite unusual," Grace said, aware he was waiting for her to ask what a sanguine was, and what special uses they had for the little vials. Perversely she kept quiet, annoyed with his supercilious manner.

Robert turned toward the bar, gesturing to the bartender. After placing his order, he turned back to Grace. His tone was more natural now and she realized he was probably just an insecure young man eager to impress her. He said, "So what brings you here tonight? Idle curiosity? Who brought you? Did you get to see the bloodletting demonstration?"

"Regan brought me. Regan Flambert. Well, her real name is Susan, but she prefers Regan. Do you know her?" As Robert shook his head, she continued, "Well, we both went to the same college and now we both work for the same law firm. We share an interest in vampires. I mean, she's really into it, all the online role-play and stuff. I guess my interest is more academic. The history of it and all."

"Role-play," he mused. "I see." Robert sipped his martini, looking her over. Grace was dressed up herself, though she wasn't sporting a cape or plastic vampire fangs. Her auburn hair was pulled back in a French braid, and her face, always pale, looked paler still, offset against her red lips.

She was dressed simply in a black silk dress, cut high at the throat and clinging elegantly to her long, thin body. It fell to the calf, though now over her crossed legs, the long slit in the fabric showing her smooth thigh.

Robert boldly took appraisal of her, his eye following the line of her dress, past the high, firm breasts, the flat belly, the long smooth legs. She felt herself blush slightly and shifted, turning away from him a little. She was extremely conscious of her thinness but had no idea of her own beauty. He smiled, narrowing his eyes. "So I gather you regard this Coven Ball as just a bunch of playacting fools gathered together to dress up and bare their fangs and say, 'I vant to suck your blood'." He spoke the last words in a heavily accented voice, obviously trying to sound like Bela Lugosi in an old Dracula film.

Grace laughed. "Something like that," she admitted. "I mean, no offense! It's fine. There's nothing wrong with it. Regan lives for these parties. You should hear her talk!"

"Your friend Regan obviously knows nothing about it," Robert interjected, as if she had challenged him. "On the surface, these Coven Balls are parties, she is right. But they are much more than that, if you know what you're looking for. There are many vampire circles or covens. These gatherings are a chance for the different covens to meet and exchange ideas. To connect with other vampires. I'll grant you, many of the people here are playacting, as you call it. Dressing up." He leaned over her conspiratorially, so she could smell the vodka on his breath. "But there are real vampires among us. There are people here from all over the country, even the world. New Orleans has long been a haven for vampires. My circle, the Red Covenant, is based here in New Orleans, but we have branches elsewhere."

"And I suppose that you're a *real* vampire?" Grace blurted, the disbelief evident in her voice. Could this guy be serious? There was no such thing as vampires, except in myth and ancient legends. Who was this guy kidding? And yet, even as these thoughts flickered through her mind, the scent of lemon and lust wafted past her, making her sit up straighter, licking her lips in anticipation of something she didn't yet understand.

"I am." Robert looked soberly proud. "I'm a sanguine vampire. That means that I need blood, human blood, to survive."

Grace's eyes widened. The constant quiet gnawing in her belly made itself known, as if his words had awakened something in herself. Robert went on, unaware of the effect his words were having. "We have all kinds of vampires in our coven. Sanguine, psychic and hybrid. As well as donors, or swans, as we call them. I am an Elder in my group, and thus am permitted to discuss the group with outsiders, or mundanes, as we call them."

Grace found Robert rather amusing and yet was intrigued despite herself. Perhaps to impress him, or because she resented his derogatory implication that she was "mundane", Grace began to talk about vampires. Not the modern-day clubs and fantasy that Robert thought of as real, but the actual history of the vampire and the associated legends and myth that had grown alongside it, becoming entangled, so that one no longer could distinguish the fact from the folklore. Her own years of casual study in the libraries of several universities had unearthed all sorts of esoteric knowledge that she now shared, in a summary fashion, with this Dracula-caped young man in white face paint.

Robert nursed his drink, at first interrupting, but then quieting as she warmed to her topic—her favorite topic, after all. When she paused to sip her own drink, he said, "You have surprised me, my lady, I confess. I took you for a fledgling, but clearly you are no novice, at least not to the history and story of our kind."

"Robert," Grace said, her natural inclination to be polite giving way at last. "Forgive me, but you can't actually be serious. 'Our kind?' Do you truly believe you are a vampire? How can you honestly think that you are one of them? I don't think they even exist anymore. It's been hundreds of years since any properly documented sightings have occurred. Even if vampires did still exist, how could you possibly claim to be one?"

Robert's countenance darkened. "We are always doubted by the mundanes. It has been ever thus." Again, she was forced to suppress a grin at his stilted language style. "I don't have to explain myself to you. But since you are so learned in our ways, I will deign to continue." The man was too silly. And yet, for some reason, she wanted to hear more. He continued, "I was 'awakened'. It happened when I was sixteen. My latent vampirism came to the fore. As I told you, I need human blood. I crave it."

Grace flashed back suddenly to her own pubescent yearnings but shook her head, banishing the thoughts.

"Well, how do you get it? Do people line up to donate? Is there a vampire blood bank, and you make deposits and withdrawals?"

"Sneer all you like. As I already mentioned, we have our donors, our swans. These are humans, mere mortals, who share their life energy without obligation. Many donors enter into partnerships with vampires. These partnerships are often also sexual in nature, although they don't have to be."

He peered now at Grace, licking his lips a little as he eyed her breasts. Grace flushed as he continued to lecture. "Many swans prefer to be monogamous, offering themselves to just one vampire at a time. Some swans will offer themselves to entire covens, provided their offerings are appreciated and not abused.

"In fact, we are meeting next Saturday. My coven that is, the Red Covenant. I am willing to allow your presence, if you care to attend. Perhaps you would even like to be a donor? To spill a little life's essence for those with whom you claim such fascination?"

He slipped a card from a little case in his pocket. Taking a pen, he wrote something on the back and then handed it to Grace. Numbly she took the little white card. She was being invited to watch people suck each other's blood. To participate, if she had a mind. The years of "academic interest" suddenly seemed to be falling away, tattering like ripped curtains against the window of her denial. The gnawing in her belly was a sharp bite now, instead of the usual dull pain.

The chance to taste it again! The sweet, heady nectar. There seemed to be no oxygen in the room suddenly. She had to get out of here. She'd been here long enough. Why had she even come? This man's offering now frightened her, as it threatened to burst open a dam of blocked feelings and needs.

Standing, she said, "I'm not well. Forgive me." Indeed, she was even paler than usual, the skin beneath her eyes looking bruised. She swayed slightly on her high heels. Robert looked concerned, dropping for the moment his persona of Lord Vampire. Solicitously he asked if he might escort her home, but she shook him off.

"No, no, thank you. I live close by." The room was closing in upon her. She had to get outside to the moist, fresh air. "Please tell my friend Regan that I had to leave." She clutched the little card in her sweaty palm.

"Call me!" Robert shouted after her, as Grace literally ran from the room. He no longer sounded like the pompous Elder of some secret blood cult. He sounded like a young man with a crush on a young woman who might be stepping out of his life forever.

But she wasn't. Far from it. She knew, even as she hurried to her little apartment on Washington Avenue, that she would be there, at the next meeting of the Red Covenant. And it wouldn't be as a donor. No. She was going to taste human blood again at last.

Chapter Four

Robert Dalton – Elder, Coven of the Red Covenant. It was neatly inscribed on one side of the card. On the other, in a thin angular scrawl he had written, *124 Charles Street. Saturday, 9:00 p.m.* Beneath it was a telephone number.

Grace fingered the little card. It was printed on fine, heavy stock, the lettering engraved in embossed shiny red. She was lying in her daybed, staring out the window. Her room was hot, despite the best efforts of the ceiling fan overhead. The little window-unit air conditioner in the adjoining room was wheezing its best effort to cool the place, but the tropical summer balm of New Orleans won out.

Grace sat in her panties and bra, her elegant black dress and high-heeled sandals tossed aside. Lifting her heavy French braid, she piled it on top of her head a moment, letting the wet breeze from her open window blow gently against her neck. The thick, waxy leaves of the magnolia tree outside her window were dripping with the recent rain shower. She'd just missed getting wet as she hurried home from the party, her mind reeling, her heart racing.

Why was she acting this way? It certainly wasn't Robert Dalton. While reasonably attractive—he was not her type. She preferred a more restrained sort of person. Someone more modest and less ostentatious.

No, it wasn't the man.

It was what he had offered.

She knew it was ridiculous. Why was she now suddenly allowing adolescent fantasies to run amuck in her head this way? She'd held such a tight rein for so long on feelings she had almost come to believe were nothing more than the feverish imagination of a young girl.

What had he said? "To spill a little of life's essence." Yes! That's what she felt now. A desperate longing for some of that promised "essence". Her own essence was flattened, she felt—a dried and sputtering spirit, left starving and hollow from years of denial and neglect. His one whisper of the chance for blood had set her body trembling, aching for it.

Yet, surely it was all a game? How could it be more? What was wrong with her? Had she read so many tomes about the creatures of the night that now she actually believed she was one? Ridiculous! Even if they did still exist, surely she would have known such a thing about herself. It would have manifested itself before now. Where were her fangs? The elongated canines reported in legend and exploited in Hollywood movies?

Parting her lips, gingerly she touched the pointed little teeth that could pierce skin and sinew with ease, if she were a real vampire. Lifting a thin white wrist, she bit gently against it, wondering what it would be like to actually puncture another's flesh. To pierce the vein and watch the glorious red tide flow from it, waiting for her special kiss. Was it her imagination, or did her canine teeth suddenly seem longer, sharper?

A bottle of wine stood next to her bed. A half-full bottle of cabernet sauvignon she'd grabbed from the kitchen counter on her way to her bed. She pulled out the cork and poured a glass. Lifting the glass goblet, she tilted her head back to take a long, deep drink, savoring its sweet burn.

Grace sighed, the image of a pale throat offered sliding unbidden into her consciousness, even as her fingers slipped down to her panties. She finished the glass and poured another, drinking it quickly. She realized she wanted to be drunk. To give herself permission in this way to do what she knew she was about to do.

So tight had been her own censorship of her true feelings that she rarely allowed herself the fantasy that was now stealthily easing its way into her brain. That pale throat, bared for her. Dark black hair curled in tendrils around it. The throat was strong, sinewy with corded muscle. It was a man's throat. Whose it was did not matter. It was an image that had floated through her dreams many times before.

Only now did she allow it to come through her conscious thought. She focused on it, imagining the face that would go with such a sensual and exposed throat. A strong jaw, a cruel mouth, but softened when it smiled. Lips ruby red, parting, revealing the elongated canines of her lover...

Her lover! Grace's fingers found their mark now, pushing aside the silky fabric of her panties. Her pussy was wet, eager for her touch. She rubbed and swirled in little arcs against her sex, moving toward the center and then away, wishing it was someone else's touch.

The wine coursed through her veins, giving her permission to explore the secret fantasy more fully. Recalling a half-forgotten dream, Grace closed her eyes. The dream brightened—its colors and feelings vivid in her mind's eye. It became more real than her narrow daybed in her small apartment, or her simple, rather dull life. For just that moment she didn't feel weak or in pain.

She could almost smell her lover now — the scent of exotic lemony spices and heat she'd experienced at the Vampire Ball. The lover of her dreams — with his dark hair and cruel smile.

They were naked, lying together on a large featherbed in the middle of a dark warm forest. He was leaning up on one elbow, kissing her hair, her forehead, her cheekbones, her lips. Slowly she felt his soft mouth edge down toward her throat.

Her golden auburn hair was loose around her head. She moved it herself, giving him access, desperate for what he was going to do. *Yes,* she thought now, *yes, do it. Take me. Claim me. I want it.* Grace moaned aloud as she rubbed herself, slipping a finger into her cunt as the dream image of her lover bit her neck, making her gasp.

He suckled at her throat, pressing his long body against hers. She shifted, her mouth watering, as she smelled her own blood on his lips. Silently she told him it was her turn, and he lay back, baring his own throat for her. She leaned over, dropping her head down, covering his face with her hair as she licked his supple flesh. In her fantasy she bit down, while in real life she only moaned, writhing against her own fingers, the sweet rusty taste of blood almost real to her.

As her sharp little teeth pierced the flesh, the impossibly rich red blood gushed like two little fountains of life against her mouth. She pulled back, trying to catch the flow, not wanting to waste a drop of his essence. It tasted better than anything she'd ever experienced in real life. It was more than drink, more than food. It went beyond mere sustenance. It was, quite literally, her life's blood.

Oh! It felt so real, just for that moment.

With a cry she came, jerking in uncontrollable little spasms, as her fingers drew out the last bit of pleasure. She fell on her side and her hand flew out to steady herself, knocking the bottle of wine from its perch, and onto her white sheets. The wine spread in a dark red pool. Grace didn't see—she was asleep, lost in blood-drenched dreams.

* * * * *

Julian moved swiftly through the throng now, trying to catch the scent again, without success. Whoever or whatever had been here had vanished. Julian felt an actual physical pain, like an ache in his chest at the loss.

Foolish man, he admonished himself. It was probably nothing more than someone's perfume. They could do anything with scents these days. But he knew he was lying to himself. Something had been there. Someone. He would stay in this town a while longer at least, and see if he couldn't discover its source. He had nothing, if not time.

Sighing a little, he consciously rearranged his features, smoothing the troubled thoughts from his mind. This was after all a gala event. The ball had reached its zenith, with many couples twirling and dancing in the center of the room to music played by a reasonably decent jazz band, which periodically exploded into Zydeco.

Julian allowed the sound to wash over him. He infinitely preferred this colorful music that evolved from the Creoles in the '30s and '40s to the technobabble that had been blasted from the speakers before this new band took the floor. The beat shifted from the two-beat Zydeco riff to a twelve-bar blues and Julian found himself swaying to the compelling rhythms.

Moving to the bar, he decided to take some refreshment. He didn't actually need food and drink to survive, but his body would tolerate it, and he could digest and excrete it the same as any human. He had found over the years that very few foods actually tempted him though he did enjoy a fine wine. Champagne remained his weakness, reminding him of his father's vineyards of long ago. The bartender seemed impressed with his choice as he popped the cork expertly into his waiter's towel and poured some wine into a chilled fluted glass. As Julian savored the tart explosion of bubbles against his tongue, he leaned against the bar, lifting a black-booted foot to press against it for balance.

Three young women approached him, giddy with drink, their faces flushed, their eyes bright. His eye was drawn to their pretty throats and he licked his lips, aware of his own constant pulse of desire.

Suppressing it, he lifted his glass toward them in greeting and smiled. "Good evening, ladies," he said, his French accent only very slight. "What are you drinking?"

"Oh! Are you buying?" one of them said, leering suggestively at him. She was young, perhaps mid-twenties, with short-cropped hair dyed an unnatural black. Her face was heavily powdered—no doubt to create the impression that she was a "creature of the night". It was a sweet face, if a little plump, and her large blue eyes would have been pretty, once the heavy black makeup that ringed them was removed. As it was, she resembled nothing so much as a raccoon.

"It would be my pleasure," Julian responded gallantly. What the hell? He was here—why not see what the night held? He wouldn't take blood tonight. Not now that he had decided to stay in this city for a while. No point in arousing suspicions. The taking of blood would be carefully planned. He would find someone homeless. Someone who, if they were coherent enough to report it wouldn't be believed—just the drunken ramblings of another crazy street person.

No, no blood tonight. But one of these three young women might provide some diversion at least. Their nubile bodies were fairly bursting from their tight, black garments. Their expressions as they gave him the once-over spoke clearly of their own wanton desires. Why not a bit of gratuitous sex?

"Well, in that case, I'll have a Bloody Mary," said the girl, who introduced herself as Tina. The other two girls both asked for rum and cola, a drink that Julian abhorred, though of course he refrained from comment.

As they clustered around him, Tina said, "I don't remember seeing you at any of the other events this year. Are you new to the area? Or did you fly in for the Ball? This is just the hottest Vampire Ball, don't you think? I play on the Masquerade site and I got a personal invitation from an Elder of the Red Star House, who actually plays online, too! How about you? Who invited you?"

Julian murmured something vague about some coven or other and she seemed satisfied with his answer. He realized she was already rather drunk and he offered an arm as she hoisted herself onto a tall stool. He noticed that she lifted her long black skirt as she sat, so that her bare skin was against the leather. The image appealed to him, even if the girl didn't.

Amy and Marguerite were happy to stand, with Marguerite edging closer and closer to Julian until her large breasts pressed against his arm. She kept her eyes leveled at his face as if completely unaware of the proximity of their bodies. Julian could smell her sweat, but it wasn't unpleasant. It mingled with baby powder and cheap perfume. He found her endearing in her earnest attempts to act innocent as she rubbed against him like a cat in heat.

They chatted about online vampire role-playing sites. Amy confided to the others that she knew of several "real" vampires here tonight. This was just a cover for the *real* gathering of the true creatures of the night.

"Oh, really?" Julian said, feigning an interest more casual than he felt. Might that presence, that other, be part of the gathering? It wasn't unheard of for actual vampires to infiltrate these clubs. He had done it himself over the years. What better place to find humans eager to share their blood, without the need for subterfuge and stolen kisses?

"And where do these *real* creatures of the night meet, Amy?"

"Well, no one knows for sure. I mean, it's a carefully guarded secret, of course. They can't have just anyone waltzing in on their secret affairs, now can they? I've heard though—" she leaned forward conspiratorially, " — that Jason's Blood Bar is a favorite haunt." She paused expectantly. "Get it? Haunt!" Her shrill laughter rang out, making Julian wince slightly.

"Of course, no one knows exactly where the blood bar is, or if it even exists! All very hush-hush, only for those real vampires in the know."

"Oh, it's real all right. I know someone who goes there regularly." Marguerite spoke, for the first time, and her voice was low and gravely in a pleasing, sexy sort of way. The other two girls whipped their faces toward her expectantly.

Marguerite smiled slightly, pleased with the attention of the group, but her eyes were only on Julian. She smiled a lazy, slow smile and said, "Yes, Becky Donovan is a donor there. She told me. It's for members only and very secretive. They serve stored blood there, and they also have willing donors, like Becky, on hand. Of course, it's completely illegal. The place doesn't have a sign, but I'm pretty sure it's in the French Quarter. Becky won't say exactly—she's sworn to secrecy." The other two young women nodded sagely. This was all such a delicious game!

"I think it's somewhere near Bourbon and Canal. I followed her once, but she saw me and wouldn't go any further until I went away." Marguerite was warming to her topic. "She was mortified that I had figured out what she was doing. She's a known donor among the various covens in the area. She gets off on it, sexually, you know?" Marguerite turned toward Julian, as if to gauge his reaction. He smiled and pressed very lightly back against her breasts still nestled at his arm. Marguerite flushed slightly but continued, "She says she can orgasm from someone sucking the blood from her arm or shoulder. She says it's this amazing sexual high for her. And at the blood bar, she gets paid, too. Pretty good gig, if you like that sort of thing."

She gazed at Julian through lowered lashes. He felt her desire like a tangible thing. He would have her tonight, if he wished. "And you, Marguerite. Are you a donor?"

"I guess that all depends on what I'm being asked to donate." She laughed a low, seductive laugh, her meaning clear, her nipples now erect against his arm. She was definitely the best looking of the three and clearly willing. He liked the way she licked her full lips, running her tongue in a circle over the top and then bottom lip in a sexy little arc. He liked her smell, something vanilla and her own animal scent.

The other two girls were pressing in now, too, showing no signs of disappearing. But Julian had picked his mate for the night. He would take her back to his lavish suite at the Worthington. Though he wasn't averse to the occasional ménage, these other two specimens held little allure. As they preened in front of him, he decided to take matters discreetly into his own hands.

Look at those two handsome men over there. They are for you. They want you. You are the chosen ones tonight. They are real vampires. They are sending telepathic messages to you. You are falling under their control. Look at them. They want you. They long for you. Julian sent these thoughts into the minds of the impressionable young women. With one accord, their heads swiveled toward the two young men Julian had chosen on a whim to be their partners.

Reasonably good-looking, the guys were gesturing toward one another, sloshing their beers as they spoke animatedly about something. They didn't seem the slightest bit interested in or even aware of Amy and Tina.

Julian turned his thoughts toward them—easily penetrating their simple and somewhat inebriated minds. After a moment both men turned toward Tina and Amy, smiles curving their lips, lust lighting their eyes. *They want to fuck you. Their names are Amy and Tina. They've been waiting all night for you to notice them. They want you. They will approach you if you just give them a signal. Raise your hands and wave them over. Take them home and they will spread their legs for you.*

Both men raised their hands, uncertainly at first, then in eager waves as Tina and Amy smiled widely at them. "Tina! They've seen us! They're real vampires!"

"Oh, my God! Amy! They're waving to us! They want us to come over! Oh, my God! Wait'll they hear about this on my site!"

Completely forgetting Julian and Marguerite, the two girls drifted away, breathlessly whispering to one another as they approached the two chosen ones. Chosen by Julian, and then forgotten as he now turned his full attention to the third young woman.

"Wow. That was weird. Tina and Amy just went off with those two guys!"

"How convenient for us, hmm?" Julian said, pressing his strong forearm against her breasts and locking eyes with her.

"Oh," Marguerite said. She licked her lips, and Julian noticed they were chapped, the red flecks of her lipstick spread unevenly against the dry mouth. He resisted a sudden impulse to bite those plump lips.

You want to leave with him. He sent the thought to her mind but really, he needn't have. Marguerite seemed quite eager of her own accord to leave the ball with a man she'd only met a few minutes before. With barely a wave to her girlfriends, Marguerite turned toward Julian and said, "So, Mr. Vampire. Do you want to suck my blood?"

"Pardon?" Julian glanced sharply at her, but saw she was merely offering what she thought was expected, as this was, after all, a party of vampires.

Marguerite giggled and said, "I'm just teasing, silly! Unless you really do? I mean, I don't do that. I just play online, you know, for fun. I don't get into that blood-play stuff."

"Of course, of course," Julian nodded, his tone soothing. "Don't worry, Marguerite, it's not your blood I want." He slipped his arm around her, leading her out into the foyer of the ballroom. As they approached the exit, a doorman hurried over, opening the large door, letting in the wet night air.

"Taxi, sir?"

"Yes, thank you." As the man hailed a cab from the waiting line of taxis, Julian turned toward the young woman. "I'm staying at the Worthington. Would you like to come to my rooms?" He'd found with women like Marguerite a direct approach was best. He didn't send her any telepathic messages encouraging a positive response. He wanted to see if she would come of her own accord.

She didn't disappoint. "Rooms! Oooh, how fancy! Does that mean like a whole suite? What are you, some kind of millionaire businessman or something?"

"No, no, just a traveler, passing through." He opened the taxi door for her, and Marguerite slipped in, revealing a long smooth thigh, as her black dress slit was pulled apart. Julian slid in next to her and said, "The Worthington." The drive was a short one, but Marguerite lost no time, placing her hand on Julian's leg and letting her red-tipped fingers trail up his strongly muscled thigh. Julian didn't stop her.

When her hand came to a rest on his crotch, he felt the responding swell of his manhood. She was leaning against his shoulder, and her cleavage presented itself alluringly to his gaze. Her breasts were large and he imagined the nipples would be generous. *She would do very nicely*, he thought.

Once in the suite, Marguerite suddenly seemed almost shy. She stood uncertainly in the middle of the sunken living room, looking around her with her arms clutched protectively around her midriff. Julian realized she must be rather young, perhaps younger than he had thought.

"How old are you?" he asked, his voice gentle.

"Nineteen." Marguerite tossed her dark hair, staring at Julian with a belligerent expression. "Plenty old enough, if that's what you're thinking."

"Indeed," Julian smiled, thinking her remark revealed just the opposite. But who was he to argue? He needed some pussy and here it was. She was only a little younger than he had been when Adrienne had bestowed her fatal kiss.

"Would you care for a drink? I have a nice bottle of champagne chilling."

"Yes. Yes, I would like that." Marguerite giggled and twirled around, still hugging herself. "That would be grand, monsieur."

"Ah, parlez vous Français, mademoiselle?" Julian gestured toward the large sofa and Marguerite flopped down upon it.

"Uh, oui, un peu, bien sûr!" Marguerite grinned, clearly pleased with herself as Julian handed her a glass of bubbly dry wine. "I *knew* you were French! I told the girls!" Marguerite quickly downed the glass and held it out for more. Julian obliged and she drained the second glass as well. Gently, Julian eased the goblet from her hand and set in on the side table next to the couch.

Marguerite giggled, finding her courage in the alcohol. She pressed her arms against her breasts, creating an even more marked cleavage. As Julian's gaze shifted to her chest, she smiled slyly — no doubt aware of the effect she was creating.

Pretending to be unaware, she went on, "You don't have much of an accent, but there's something about you. Something European. Something exotic. Something," she paused, cocking her head slightly as she eyed the vampire, "something dangerous."

Julian's eyes darkened as she spoke. He felt his bloodlust rise. If she had any idea of the potential danger she was in, she would probably faint away on the spot, or more likely, run screaming from the room. Just one kiss with his sharp teeth against her supple throat, and he could kill her, sucking enough blood from her to leave her lifeless in a matter of minutes.

The room seemed to close in on Julian for a moment. He felt dizzy with need, an aching, palpable need for human blood. Swallowing, he took a deep breath, closing his eyes as he willed himself to resist the call of her blood.

The room seemed to recede back to normal proportions. His head cleared, and he shook his long hair away from his face. He stared at the young woman who had helped herself to a third glass of champagne. Her legs were crossed so that her broad thigh was fully revealed to his gaze. She wore no stockings.

So young! So ripe for the taking. And yet, he had promised himself he would bide his time in this sultry town. He would not use her for her blood. No, he would wait, and instead take his fill of her round and willing young body.

He settled next to Marguerite on the couch. Placing his arm around her, he let his hand fall to her ample right breast, which was already mostly exposed by her closefitting, low-cut gown. His long fingers slipped easily past the black material and lifted the breast from her dress.

"Hey," Marguerite protested, but weakly, as he found a large nipple and rolled it between thumb and finger, quickly bringing it to an engorged state so that it resembled a fat little pencil eraser.

Bending over her, Julian licked her neck, tasting her sweat and young sweetness. Marguerite shivered and said, "Hey," again, as he began to kiss her throat while his hand sought the other breast, pulling it free as well.

"So are you like a real vampire?" she murmured against his hair. Julian barely heard her. He was intent upon slipping her dress from her body. Marguerite said again, "Hey, Julian, are you like a real vampire? You know, that sucks blood? I said before I wasn't into it? But you know I'm awfully curious. I've thought about being a donor, you know. Letting someone do it to me."

"You don't know what you're talking about." Julian knelt down in front of the young woman, whose face was flushed. She'd had three glasses of the champagne in quick succession, on top of whatever she had been drinking at the party.

Julian had no intention of doing the gallant thing and taking her home. He was going to fuck her. He was going to use her until he used her up. He felt his balls tighten as he leaned over her bared breasts and bit her nipples. Marguerite moaned and let her head fall back, revealing her plump white throat. To distract himself from that offering, Julian again focused on her breasts, biting her nipple harder this time, so that Marguerite yelped a little. He pulled at the nipple, forcing it to distend even further.

"Ouch!" Marguerite squealed, trying to sit up. "Hey, you're hurting me."

Julian was breathing hard. He released her nipple but only to bite the other one, just as hard. The young woman pushed against his broad shoulders with her hands, trying to push him off her.

He yielded, standing up. Leaning down Julian pulled at Marguerite's arms, forcing her to stand. "Look at you," he said, his eyes flashing. "You look like a slut, Marguerite. Your breasts exposed, your hair wild about your face. I must have you, girl. Now."

Without waiting for her reaction, indeed not caring how she reacted, Julian swept the girl up and tossed her easily over his shoulder. Marguerite pummeled his back halfheartedly, but to no avail.

Walking into the bedroom, he threw the girl down on the king-sized bed. "Don't move," he commanded, his voice no longer gentle.

"Hey, listen, you're scaring me, cut it out," Marguerite said, half sitting up. Julian cocked his head toward her. He could feel her fear. She wasn't lying. But he could also smell her lust. She was redolent with it, and he knew if he put his hand on her sex, it would come away wet with her desire.

He pulled off his pants and stripped off his shirt, revealing his hard, smooth body. His cock was so erect it was peeking over the top of his silk bikini briefs. His head was pounding with lust now. If only he could have it all! If only he could suck her blood while he fucked her! How sublime that would be. And yet, he knew she couldn't withstand it. Whatever silly fantasies she entertained about being a "donor", she had no idea what she was offering.

Only another vampire could withstand that kind of lovemaking. Julian's thoughts flitted to the last time he was with another vampire. Many years had passed since that sharing of the blood, that dance on the edge of oblivion. The mere act of making love could turn dangerous between vampires. Too often, they were seized with a bloodlust so fierce that they were unable to stop the exchange. With their mouths on each other's throats and their bodies locked together, their blood would flow between them until they finally fell apart, exhausted and wasted. Uncontrolled, the event took a huge toll, even on the strongest vampire. The sacred sharing of the blood was not for the weak.

Marguerite was only a fragile human who would surely die from a vampire's kiss. Tonight she would only taste his lips and his cock. Even this was a sweet temptation, and Julian smiled a wolf's grin as he contemplated the waiting girl lying helpless on the bed before him, her breasts still lewdly exposed over the top of her low-cut gown.

He would try not to hurt her, but his lust was rising, and Julian was not gentle by nature. He liked to take his wenches by force. He liked the thrill of fear in their eyes when he revealed his huge cock, which he did now, stripping off his underwear and letting his sizable endowment spring free.

Marguerite gasped and shifted on the bed, but Julian was upon her, pulling at the zipper at the back of her dress, and then pulling it over her head in a tumble of hair and arms. With one strong hand, he pulled off her little panties, which were indeed wet at the crotch.

"Please! This is too fast! Please! I'm not on the pill!"

"Hush," Julian tried to control his raging desire. All he wanted was to plunge himself into her—to rip her in half with his cock, and use her until she cried. But while he liked a little fear, he also wanted desire. A rape without mutual lust and attraction held no appeal, and so he forced himself to slow down, and calm the young woman trembling naked on the bed in front of him.

"Marguerite, my love. You are so beautiful. I can barely contain my desire for you. Ma chère. Ma petite belle chère. You know you need this. I'll be gentle. I must have you! And don't worry about getting with child. I, alas, am sterile. I cannot make a baby, even if I wished to. So calm your fears. Spread your beautiful legs and let me taste you."

Kneeling at the edge of the bed, he nuzzled his face near her spread pussy. The heady musk of her sex filled his nostrils, and he licked at the delicate folds, stilling at last her protests. Marguerite moaned, thrusting herself up against his mouth. Not all women were so eager for this kiss, and from a veritable stranger at that. Julian was pleased that he had pegged this woman as the slut she clearly was.

He licked and teased her until she was crying the words he wanted to hear. "Fuck me! Fuck me! Do it!" Marguerite grunted, pulling Julian up by his thick dark hair. He lifted himself over her and plunged his rock-hard cock into her slick opening, not caring now if he hurt her, only wanting to be enveloped in her hot, tight warmth.

Grabbing her soft breasts, he kneaded and pinched her flesh, biting his own lips to keep from biting her throat. How he longed to bury his fangs along that sweet pulse in her neck, to taste the rich, delicious offering that coursed through her veins.

He would do it! It had been so long! Take the blood offering. Suck her dry. Ease his own gnawing hunger! Why not? She was just a human. A frail, useless human with only a few natural years to live. Why not take her now? Who would know? He could disappear, leave this city and drift again, perhaps back to Europe.

Marguerite was moaning now, screaming her pleasure as he rammed his cock deep inside of her. She clutched his neck, wrapping her legs around his hips to pull him even deeper into her. Julian opened his eyes, seeing her face, a young face still barely defined, cheeks still rounded in innocence. Would he take that life? Snuff out her essence with one greedy kiss?

She cried out now, "Julian, Julian! Yes! Yes, yes, yes!" She spasmed against him, jerking for several seconds. Her dark eyes slowly opened, unfocused at first. The mascara was smeared down one cheek. Slowly she smiled, and then covered his face in a myriad of tiny kisses that suddenly broke his heart. Sweet, trusting girl, bestowing those little kisses on the being who was contemplating her death while he fucked her.

Focusing instead on her hot cunt still wrapped around his cock, Julian moved inside of her, creating the needed friction to come, which he did, arching against her, his eyes squeezed shut, his mouth pressed closed to keep from offering that fatal kiss.

As he lay, his heart pounding against hers, Julian moaned softly. His cock at least was satisfied for the moment, but he knew it wouldn't be long before he would be forced to take some blood. New Orleans was going to taste the kiss of a vampire.

Chapter Five

Saturday morning dawned in typical fashion, humid and hinting of the heat to come. Grace lay naked on her bed — the sheets twisted around her legs, watching the sky darken from palest pink to watery blue. The heady perfume from the magnolia blossoms wafted through the screen window. The thick creamy petals were wilting, turning brown at the edges in the hot Louisiana sun.

Grace fingered the little card she'd kept on her nightstand since she'd fled the Vampire Ball the week before. She'd tried to ignore it, focusing on her daily duties at work and her usual routines at home. She hadn't succeeded. It almost seemed animate — whispering as she passed by.

Now that the day had come at last, she'd picked it up again, reading the bold red embossed letters on the front, *Robert Dalton — Elder, Coven of the Red Covenant.* Flipping it over, she read the words that were already memorized, *124 Charles Street. Saturday, 9:00 p.m.*

He had said to call him. Did that mean she needed to call and confirm her attendance at this thing, whatever it was? This meeting of the chosen few. Of the "real" vampires who were going to partake in silly little blood rituals, pretending they were something that couldn't be real?

Yet, who was she to put it down? Especially when just the thought of human blood now sent a fierce jolt of desire zinging through her? How had she denied it for so many years? And why now had the layers of denial and protection seemed to fall away like discarded garments?

She would go. Not that this was a new decision. She had decided from the moment he'd handed her his card that she would go. Only now, she was finally admitting it definitively to herself. Yes, she would go.

Robert had seemed surprised but pleased when she'd telephoned. He'd given her directions which she didn't need, having found occasion several times over the past week to wander by the address, not far from her own.

The house was an old colonial-style mansion, in a state of semi-disrepair, but still grand in its own right. Several large weeping willows graced its front lawn. Robert had told her he lived there with several other members of the coven. "It was my grandfather's," he had remarked proudly. "And now it's mine. The entire estate went to me, as the last surviving heir." *I'm rich* was the underlying subtext but Grace, who had never much cared about material things, hadn't been particularly impressed.

Now as she walked down the old cobbled walk to the door her legs felt boneless and her mouth was dry. What was she doing? Something compelled her forward and she found herself at the door, a massive oak affair with an old-fashioned knocker positioned in the center. It was 9:15, as Grace hadn't wanted to be the first one to arrive.

A nondescript young woman in a black blouse and black jeans opened the door. She was barefoot, and her long blonde hair was pulled away from her face. Grace suddenly felt overdressed in her silk, sleeveless blouse and narrow skirt that tapered just below her knee.

"Come in, you must be Grace!" The young woman smiled, showing uneven teeth and dimpled cheeks. Her voice was kind and welcoming, and Grace felt one of the little knots of uncertainty in her gut unwind.

"I'm Rhonda. I'm a swan. Uh, a donor. Robert's told me about you. He says you're new to the scene, but very learned in the lore. A scholar, he said."

"Oh, well," Grace said, not sure how to respond.

Rhonda led Grace into a large living room. It was full of comfortable old furniture covered in faded, dark pink velvet. Plump sofas and chairs were distributed about the room and the floors were covered in faded Oriental carpets rubbed threadbare in patches but still quite beautiful. Huge oil paintings graced the walls, depicting scenes of old New Orleans and the Mississippi as well as portraits of dowagers and dignitaries now long forgotten.

Robert was sitting with a small group of people. He turned his head as they entered and stood up quickly, smoothing his hair back with one hand. "Grace! You came. I'm so pleased. I've told the others about you, and they are looking forward to meeting you. Come, let me introduce you."

Grace met several unremarkable people. As she shook one hand after the other, she realized she felt rather let down. She'd been expecting a production, she realized, more along the lines of the Vampire Ball, with costumes and blood dripping from fangs.

Robert placed his hand proprietarily on Grace's back as he led her to a large chair, pressing her shoulder lightly to indicate that she should sit. "Today we're going to perform a cutting. Our swans are going to give us their blood. We have three swans here today — Rhonda, whom you've met, as well as Gina and Mark. Gina belongs to the coven at large. That is, we all share her. Rhonda — " he patted Rhonda's arm as she smiled up at him, " — is owned by me and Mark serves Mistress Margo. And this is Frank, one of our select sanguines."

Grace stared at the donors. Gina, a little woman of barely five feet, was perched on the knee of Frank, a slightly balding man with a kind face. Mark was standing behind his mistress' chair, a hand lightly on her shoulder. He looked to be in his mid-thirties and his most striking feature was a full head of bright yellow-blond hair.

Mistress Margo was striking, with dark hair streaked with lines of pure silver. Her eyes were a rich brown, set against olive-toned skin. She was dressed in a dark leather vest and pants. She wore no shirt beneath it and her cleavage was pronounced. Grace noticed that Mark wore the same outfit, his arms bare and thick blond hair curling up at the top of his vest.

"And you, Grace? Would you like to be a swan today? Or are you more interested in tasting the sweet offering? You must choose one or the other, you know. We aren't a freak show put on for your amusement." It was Margo who spoke, and her voice was rich and deep, smooth as syrup.

"Oh." Grace felt herself flush and yet her mouth was actually watering as she contemplated the offer of blood. The longing in her belly was so fierce now she had to consciously resist the urge to double over. "To taste," she whispered. Her pussy was throbbing, and she fancied for one horrible moment that the others could smell her arousal.

Margo laughed, throwing back her head theatrically. "I thought so," she nodded. "You don't have the mark of a donor, though Robert was hoping, weren't you, lad?"

Robert smiled a little, but he looked irritated. Abruptly he said, "Well then. We shall give you a demonstration, and you shall find out for yourself if you are sanguine or simply curious. Rhonda!" His voice assumed an authoritative tone as he called for her. "Come here. I'm going to use you today for our guest's pleasure."

"Yes, sir." Rhonda hurried over. Like many donors, she was sexually submissive and the giving of blood was a turn-on. With no apparent embarrassment, Rhonda stripped off her blouse, revealing her bare torso. She was small-breasted and had no need of a bra, but Grace had not been expecting the young woman to strip and she found herself blushing. No one else seemed the slightest bit concerned.

Rhonda knelt on the carpet in front of Robert. Her eyes flickered across Grace, who couldn't help but notice the soft roundness of Rhonda's little breasts, tipped with creamy brown nipples. She tried to focus as Robert said, "The important thing during a cutting is to make sure that you are both as relaxed as possible, as tension will make the incision more painful. You need to use a clean razor knife or razorblade. You choose a fleshy area such as the biceps, outer arm, thigh, calf muscle or stomach."

Robert produced a little silver razor knife and flicked up the sharp blade at its tip. "You must make sure the area is clean—" he swabbed at Rhonda's arm, as if preparing to give her a shot. "You use the blade to make a shallow incision, never deeper than the top of the fatty layer of skin, and never over a vein."

Everyone was quiet, leaning forward with their eyes on Rhonda, whose eyes were now submissively focused on the ground in front of her. If she was nervous about the fact that her flesh was about to be cut, she didn't show it.

Grace found herself clutching the arms of her chair, barely breathing. Robert took the knife, sliding it gently against Rhonda's flesh. Rhonda drew in a sharp breath, but otherwise remained still.

"You must make the cut slowly," he said, as he drew the blade down, "not too fast or sloppy. And stop if it hurts your donor too much. Rhonda can tolerate the pain, though, can't you, girl? She likes it, don't you?" His voice changed when he spoke directly to Rhonda, it was overlaid with sexual innuendo and power. Rhonda nodded slowly, still keeping her eyes to the ground. She drew her tongue slowly over her lips.

Robert turned back to his audience, clearly enjoying the attention. But Grace's eyes were on Rhonda, on her arm. A thin line of bright red no longer than an inch stood out against her triceps. Little red droplets hung suspended, and Grace actually had to resist an impulse to leap up and suck them away. She gripped the arms of her chair as she watched, riveted. Rhonda's head remained bowed but her nipples were erect, and her breathing was labored, making her little breasts rise and fall.

Robert now knelt next to Rhonda, ignoring her bare torso, focusing instead on the little cut on her upper arm. He lowered his mouth to the cut and Grace could sense his nervousness, his excitement. His eyes slid toward her as his tongue darted out for a tentative lick. Grace suddenly had the feeling he was performing. He wasn't a "vampire", he was a showman and she was his audience.

She could feel his words against her brain. *Are you impressed? Look at what I'm doing. I'm sucking someone's blood.* But her own blood-hunger superseded her awareness of the man. He was speaking again, "The trick is not to lose control and bite down, but to use a gentle, firm suction and stop after a minute or so to let more blood fill the area. If your donor feels dizzy, stop and let them lie down and quit for a while. Never take more than a mouthful or a few tablespoons total."

He covered the little cut, his head obscuring Grace's view. He sat back after a moment. Rhoda's eyes were closed and her head had fallen back. Her mouth was slack, partially open, as if she were sleeping.

"Powerful!" Robert exclaimed, looking again directly at Grace. Everyone in the little circle seemed riveted to his performance. He licked his lips, smiling at them all. Grace almost expected him to stand and take a bow. Instead, he said, "Grace, would you like to try?"

"Me?" she responded inanely.

Margo intervened. "Not yet, Robert. She's not ready to cut yet. But perhaps a taste of the life's blood would be in order. Would you like to taste, Grace?"

Grace bit her lips. Her teeth actually felt itchy. It wasn't a razor knife that she wanted to use. She wanted to bite. She wanted to bite down on the tender jugular just visible beneath the skin. God, what was happening to her! Of course, she couldn't do that. These professed vampires didn't use their teeth! Of course they didn't. All this talk of sharp blades and cleansing the area. They made it sound like a procedure in a doctor's office.

And yet, what else would they do? Grace felt so confused. Why did she have this fierce desire, this burning need, to taste that blood? How had she gone for so long resisting it, only to have it rear itself now with far more power than when she first felt the need at puberty?

"Hello, earth to Grace," Robert said impatiently. Grace realized with a start she had been daydreaming.

"Yes," she said, her voice trembling slightly, "Yes, I'd like to taste."

Robert had pressed a bandage over Rhonda's right arm. Now he moved to her other arm and flicked out the little blade. With less fanfare, he drew it across her flesh. Rhonda winced but again remained still. Grace knelt down from her chair.

She could feel her own heart hammering against her ribs. The smell of the blood hit her like something palpable. Oh, God. She had to have this. Trying to hide her brazen need, she leaned carefully toward the thin arm. A trickle of blood slid down the pale skin and Grace's tongue snaked out, eager not to miss a drop.

It melted away like the promise of freedom. She bent forward again, this time locking her mouth over the little wound. Licking across the length of it, she felt the sweet blood coat her tongue. Against her will, a little moan escaped her throat as the blood bubbled up with her gentle suck.

She swallowed, feeling the hot, sweet nectar course down her throat like something magic. For the first time since she could remember, the gnawing pain in her gut was eased. Sometimes only a whisper of discomfort, sometimes a raging ache, it had never truly left her since the onset of puberty, when she first became obsessed with all things vampire.

She exerted all her will to keep from biting. Her canines actually felt longer, sharper, against her tongue. But she knew she mustn't bite. She must control this bizarre impulse.

Grace felt a curious lightness in her limbs. She felt powerful and as if all her senses were heightened.

Suddenly she became aware of Rhonda, of Rhonda's reactions. She could sense the girl's sexual arousal. She could smell Rhonda's desire, mingling with her own. Rhonda's eyes were closed, but Grace suddenly knew, as if Rhonda had spoken aloud, that the young woman was deeply aroused by this process, in spite of the sting of the cuts on each arm, or perhaps partially because of it.

Grace knew with the part of her brain that could still think that she should sit back. Robert had intoned that she mustn't take more than a mouthful. And yet, she couldn't stop. It was good—so good. It was water to a parched desert. It was startling awareness to someone who had always lived in a kind of semi-sleep state, waiting for something that had at last arrived. She sucked harder, giving in to her own desperate craving, though still managing to keep her teeth safely tucked under her lips.

"Grace. Grace. Grace! You need to stop. Now. Grace." Dimly she became aware of the voices. And then she felt hands, strong hands but feminine ones, as Margo pulled her away from the donor. With deep reluctance, Grace yielded her hold. She felt feverish and suddenly angered that something was standing in the way of her drink.

The mist of blood-fever slowly cleared and she sat back, dazed. Her cheeks were hot, her eyes over-bright. "Jesus Christ, Robert. Where did you find this one? She is the real thing, cher. No question about it." Margo was smoothing back Grace's hair, which was matted with sweat. Gently she helped her to the couch, sitting next to her and taking her hands into her own.

Robert was staring. He seemed a little put out, as if he had been expecting a different reaction from her. Perhaps he had been hoping to impress, even to horrify a little. Instead, Grace was the one who had impressed them all.

Turning his attention to his submissive, Robert opened a little bandage, prepared to press it against the bloodied cut. Oddly, it was no longer bleeding. One could barely detect the wound! He glanced sharply at Grace, his expression confused. "Rhonda!" he barked. "You're dismissed. Put your blouse on and go wait in my room." Rhonda stood slowly, her legs shaking. The experience had clearly been an intense one for her as well. She swayed slightly, and Mark stepped over to steady her, taking gentle hold of one elbow. He walked her out of the living room. Just before she disappeared, Rhonda turned back to stare at Grace.

"I don't know what you think you were doing," Robert began, his voice injured and imperious.

"Hush, now, Robert. I don't think *she* knew what she was doing, did you, chérie? Just leave her be. Rhonda is fine. Why don't you go check on her, to make sure, Robert?" Margo's gaze was firm and Robert, his mouth crimped in a tight little line of disapproval, left the room.

Reaching toward a bowl of fruit on the low table in front of them, Margo selected a large round orange. With a little knife, she cut the thick dimpled rind, revealing the sweet fruit. Silently she handed a wedge to Grace, who took it with trembling fingers and lifted it to her lips.

Margo continued to smooth Grace's heavy hair from her pale face. Speaking softly she said, "Where have you been hiding yourself, my dear? And how long have you felt the thirst?"

Chapter Six

Marguerite stayed the night, though Julian would have preferred that she left. She was passed out in a drunken stupor and he was gentleman enough to let her be. Now that his sexual lust was satisfied for the moment, his thoughts turned back to blood.

"Marguerite," he whispered several times, but she didn't move or respond. Focusing his mind on hers, he sensed the fuzzy cotton of liquor-induced unconsciousness. She would have to sleep it off. He doubted she would stir before morning, and so he quietly dressed and left the room.

He felt no need for sleep though the hour was close to 3:00 a.m. Vampires did take rest but they needed far less than humans. And at the moment, the need for blood outweighed any fatigue. Stepping outside, Julian took a deep breath of the thick night air.

He knew that while it was safe to wander at night in the heavily populated tourist area of the French Quarter, even just a few blocks to the south would take him into dangerous neighborhoods where the ravages of crack, cocaine and poverty had created an environment that was frightening and even dangerous to the unprepared.

That was exactly where Julian wanted to go, however, as he sought out a victim. It had been too long, much too long and he couldn't wait another moment. He knew if he had stayed with Marguerite, he would kill her with his kiss.

Instead, he strode away from the bright lights of privilege and tourist attractions, walking quickly toward the loading docks on the seedier side of the riverfront. The anticipation of a blood meal made him almost dizzy with need.

It didn't take long to find what he was seeking. An old man was sleeping against the side of a warehouse, an empty bottle of vodka at his side. His head was slumped over, a soft snore issuing from his mouth. A thread of drool glistened at his lip. The old man was dark-skinned and gaunt, dressed in clothing that might have once had color, but was faded with dirt and time to a muddy gray.

Julian crouched next to the man. He stank of rank sweat and alcohol, but Julian didn't care. Kneeling close to the man, tenderly he touched his neck, feeling for the delicate pulse at his throat. He looked around but other than the two of them, the area was deserted.

As if lifting a child, Julian stood with the old man in his arms. He didn't awaken but cried out softly in his sleep, the words an unintelligible mumble. Julian moved to the side of the building, out of sight of the deserted road. He pulled the filthy old shirt from the man's body and now he did come awake, jerking his head with a slurred, "What the…"

Julian didn't bother to try and enter the man's head to calm him and make him compliant. His need was too urgent and he knew the man was too weak, and still too drunk to make any effectual protest.

He bit, his teeth sinking in past grimy flesh to the sweet, clean, hot blood within. Blood—its color the pure scarlet of the poppies that grew in the fields of his boyhood. It gushed up like a little geyser, and Julian moaned with passionate pleasure as it filled his mouth with coppery perfection.

The man fought back at first, trying to claw at Julian's arms, which were wrapped firmly around him. Julian barely noticed his impotent struggle. Soon the man fell limp as he drifted into unconsciousness from fear and loss of blood. Still Julian's mouth stayed locked on his neck.

Oh, he would stop soon. He must stop soon or the man would die. He would stop. Just a little more. Oh, just a little more.

He didn't stop.

He suckled and sucked until he had bled the man dry. Life was ripping like fire through his veins. He felt powerful and alive! He felt as if he could swallow the world whole. He felt like singing and laughing, and crying all at once. The blood-fever raged through him as he sat alone in the pre-dawn with the bone-dry hull of a man in his arms.

The fever, which had seized him, slowly ebbed as he finally sat back, his lips still stained red with blood. Without recognition, he looked down at the corpse that lay in his arms, its face gray and marked with death. The head lolled inertly as Julian shifted and he stifled a little cry of dismay.

He hadn't meant to kill the man. He had gone too long, denying his need for human blood. Now he had cost a human his life. His own primal urges had driven him to murder yet again. With a sigh he stood, letting the corpse roll gently to the ground. It was after all only a human. A sick old man with little time left and clearly nothing to hope for. Did that make it excusable? Julian sighed, and walked slowly back to his hotel ready at last to sleep.

* * * * *

Marguerite was good to her word. She had managed to arrange to take Julian to the blood bar, having apparently convinced her friend Becky to let them in on the secret. They went on Saturday night, after a week of sex, which grew increasingly dull for Julian, though poor Marguerite claimed to be falling in love.

It wasn't that he didn't like her, but she was, after all, only nineteen and they had absolutely nothing in common but the sex, and her professed interest in all things vampire. In fact, he came to learn rather quickly that her interest was completely superficial, based only on silly ideas garnered from online role-playing games.

This left only the sex, and Julian was a fickle man, preferring new conquests with trembling girls spreading their legs in a mixture of fear and lust. Marguerite had become a known quantity and not a very exciting one. He knew he would have to let her down gently, but he kept her around for the week, knowing she was the easy route to this so-called blood bar, which he was curious to visit.

What was a week after all, in the life of a vampire? Nothing at all. He told her he was leaving the city in a few days but that he would keep in touch, and they would meet again when he returned. He had no such intention, but Marguerite believed him. The relief that he would soon be rid of her, as well as the knowledge that she was young and would easily recover offset the twinge of guilt he felt at lying to her. Though she claimed otherwise, she wasn't in love with him by any stretch, but was only enjoying the amorous attentions of a mysterious older man who could fuck her senseless night after night.

"It's up here, on Bourbon. You wouldn't even notice it! I've walked past it myself. You think it's an antique shop, one that always seems to be closed. Becky showed me." She leaned toward Julian, whispering conspiratorially, "and I have the password! It's Jalena."

Julian looked sharply at the girl. Jalena! Was it a coincidence? Surely it must be. And yet—he had known Jalena. She was already an old soul when he had been turned. He'd lost track of her and Dusan at least a century ago. She had passed into legend, but she had been human once upon a time. Originally a queen of one of the many city-states that littered Europe in the twelfth century, she had been "turned" by the Elder Dusan, who had fallen in love with her. She had been dying of some fatal human disease when Dusan gave her the kiss of a vampire life. All illness fell away and their passion became legendary in the vampire world.

Enduring vampire romantic love was rare, as the population was small and scattered over the globe. Couplings did occur and even true love, as was the case between Jalena and Dusan. However these relationships rarely lasted, spanning only a hundred years or so before one or the other lost interest and moved on. Yet, these two names remained linked and they were together still, as far as Julian knew.

Marguerite of course was unaware of the impact that her password had on Julian. He was left to wonder how these humans had come across it. He wasn't really surprised, as much of the so-called vampire research contained kernels of truth, as is often the case with legends. "Here it is, 'Foulet's Antiques—Closed'," she read. "This is it!" Marguerite gripped Julian's arm and he could feel her excitement. This was all just a glorious game to her.

Julian knocked on the glass pane of the door but there was no response. Noticing a little chain dangling on the frame, he pulled it. A distant tinkling sound was heard from inside. After a moment, someone shuffled forward and unlocked the door, cracking it a bit. "We're closed for summer inventory. Go away."

"Jalena," Julian said, softly rolling the J in proper Slavic pronunciation.

"Well then," said the man, closing the door a moment so he could release the chain. He opened the door and peered nearsightedly at the two of them. The man seemed to be in his mid to late sixties, with grizzled gray hair like lamb's wool. His skin was a dark mahogany and stretched tight over the bones of his face.

Julian could feel inside the man's mind that he was weighing the two of them for worthiness. He could also sense that the man sometimes turned people away. Julian and Marguerite seemed to pass muster because after a moment, the man stood back and said, "That'll be forty dollars each. You go back through there." He pointed a bony finger toward the back room.

Julian handed over a hundred-dollar bill, waving away the man's attempt to make change. "Enjoy, enjoy," the old fellow grinned, clearly pleased with the tip. Julian knew he was assured reentry should he wish it at a later date.

They stepped through the little back door and walked down a narrow corridor, paint peeling from its walls. Julian was reminded of Prohibition, when speakeasies were the order of the day in cities like New York and Chicago. New Orleans was an exception, he recalled, pretty much ignoring Prohibition from the start, its population amused and disdainful of such a ridiculous law.

They came to the end of a hall where the words *Jason's Blood Bar* were painted in curly black letters against a red door. They stood uncertainly for a moment, and then Julian turned the handle.

Inside was dark. Julian, who could actually see better in a half-light, quickly took in his surroundings. The place was set up like a typical bar or pub, with a long, high counter complete with tall, leather barstools with chrome circles at their base for resting one's feet. The room wasn't large and the rest of it was filled with a scattering of small tables. He saw that the walls were painted a blood red. The ceiling was covered in tin tiles stamped with designs and surely dated back at least a hundred years.

But what most caught Julian's attention was the scent. The ripe, lovely smell of human blood. It was here—the place was rife with it. Even though he'd slaked his blood-thirst just a few days before, his mouth began to water. He noticed the long glass cabinets behind the bar stocked with little bottles of red liquid. Stored blood?

The bartender noticed them and came out from behind the bar, wiping his hands on his black denim jeans. He was a tall man with long, strong arms lined with thick ropy veins. His face was creased like someone who has spent a good deal of time in the sun, though he didn't look older than perhaps thirty-five. He held out his hand, his expression guarded. "I'm Jason. I don't recognize you. How, may I ask, do you come to be here?"

"Oh!" Marguerite looked frightened. She had, after all, cajoled the password out of her friend Becky. Her expression now registered that she might be regretting her decision to use it. "Gosh, I hope it's okay! I...uh...that is—"

Taking the offered hand in a firm but friendly grip Julian interrupted, "We're friends of Becky Johnson. We were told we'd receive a welcome here. I'm a sanguine vampire and my friend Marguerite is a swan." Julian knew the local lingo and didn't hesitate to add a bit of a mind-bend as he entered the man's thoughts and whispered, *These people are welcome. They are legitimate. They are safe.*

Jason's scowl slowly smoothed to a smile. "Well, all right then," he said. "Make yourself at home. I've got some excellent fresh blood tonight, just bottled. We will also have a live donor on the premises if you've a mind to do a bit of cutting. She should be coming with her coven within the hour."

Julian licked his lips, trying not to let his greed betray him. They sat at the bar, with Marguerite speaking in a loud stage whisper, "You were amazing! He bought it! Me! A swan! Imagine!"

Jason glanced at them as he stepped back behind the bar but said nothing. Julian said quietly, "I suggest you hold your tongue, Marguerite. Let's just see what the place is about, shall we?" Marguerite looked miffed, but said no more.

"What's your pleasure then, Julian?" Jason asked.

"How fresh is it?"

"About an hour old. These bottles here." He waved toward the refrigerated case. "Twenty dollars a pop. Clean donor. Eats organic foods."

Julian suppressed a grin. These modern fools with their constant food fads. He couldn't care less what they ate or drank. It made no difference to his vampire heart.

Only that the blood be human, and from a living person. He'd never tried bottled blood and doubted it would be worth much to him. Nonetheless, he was intrigued and so he said, "I'll try a bottle."

"Julian!" Marguerite nudged him sharply with her shoulder. "You're actually going to try *real* blood? Ewww!" Julian gripped her arm, pushing her elbow gently but firmly away. He shot a thought into her head, *Be still. Be quiet. Don't talk. Everything is fine. Everything is as it should be.* As he felt her relax, he let go of her arm and smiled reassuringly at her.

If Jason noticed any of this, he didn't comment, but said, "And for the lady?"

"Oh. Um. I'll have a rum and cola?"

"Sorry, we don't serve alcohol here."

"Oh," Marguerite looked genuinely nonplussed. She stared helplessly at Jason until Julian said, "How about a Virgin Mary? Would that suit you, Marguerite?"

Marguerite sighed with relief and nodded her head, "Yes, that would be perfect."

Jason placed the ridiculously small glass bottle of bright red nectar in front of Julian along with a little shot glass. Julian forgot for a moment that Marguerite was beside him. Slowly he unscrewed the little cap and lifted the bottle, tilting its contents into the glass. He had to swallow rapidly to keep from choking on his saliva as the rush of blood scent assailed his nostrils.

When Marguerite had her drink in front of her, he lifted his and nodded toward her, offering a silent toast. She watched with evident fascination as he lifted the glass to his lips and drank.

Ah. No, it wasn't fresh and hot from the veins of a living thing, but it was still delicious—piquant and delicately flavored, the blood of a woman. His hand trembled slightly as he refilled the shot glass, which resulted in emptying the little bottle. Again he drank, his bloodlust now ignited.

A mistake! He wanted more! His eyes slid feverishly over Marguerite's neck, which was fully revealed as she had pulled her hair back in a barrette that evening. Biting his lips, he dug his fingernails into his thighs, silently fighting for control. "Another!" he called to Jason, who raised his eyebrows but made no further comment.

In a moment, a second little bottle of life was set before him, and Julian drank it greedily, though he tried to make it last. He felt the pulsing throb of bloodlust in his head. His cock ached and extended as he shifted on the stool to hide his erection. "Another!" he called, his voice cracking with need.

"Sorry, pal. Two's the limit. That'll be forty bucks." Seeing Julian's countenance darken, he added, "Hey, I've got a party coming in. A coven. I only have six bottles left. What's with you, anyway? Nobody ever asks for seconds. You'd think you were a *real* vampire, for God's sake. Get a grip."

The few people at the little tables around them had grown silent. All eyes seemed to be on Julian and Jason. There was a hush as they waited to see what happened next. Julian felt a film of red hatred slide over his eyes. Rage seemed to well up from some carefully protected place. How dare this impudent human deny him his due?

Julian had never fed in front of humans before. Never in all his years wandering the globe had he partaken in the drink of life in front of them. How *dare* this ridiculous man presume to insult him by withholding what he was ready to pay for? He clenched his fists in anger. Jason stood implacable behind the bar.

"Julian," Marguerite said, her voice high pitched with nervousness, "Julian, what's gotten into you? You're acting, like, really weird, you know? Like, what is going on anyway?"

Somehow, her words penetrated his blood-rage and he felt his pounding heart returning to something like normal. The red film receded and he realized he was behaving foolishly by calling attention to himself and his need. It was over in a moment, as he regained control of his behavior.

"Sorry," he said shortly. "My mistake." Reaching for his wallet, he pulled out several twenties. "I need some air," he said to Marguerite. "You wait here. I won't be long."

Without waiting for her reply, Julian slipped away. As he stepped out of the little building, after telling the old man he'd be back in a few moments, he almost collided with a group of people dressed in black capes. He observed a tallish young man with his hair brushed straight back, an older woman though still quite beautiful, her dark hair streaked dramatically with lines of silver and a young blonde woman holding tightly to the man's arm.

As he slid past them, taking this all in at a glance, he heard the young man say, "Jalena."

Chapter Seven

This time he was quick and probably not as careful as he should have been. At least he left his victim alive and merely unconscious, slumped over against a doorframe like a common drunk. His sharp vampire's teeth slid neatly into the woman's neck, once he rendered her unconscious in a chokehold from behind. Within minutes he had sucked his fill, at least enough to get him through the evening.

His cock strained in his pants as it always did when he sucked human blood. Early on, when he was still learning his own powers and weaknesses, he had thought he could control his impulses. How divine to suck the sweet juice of life while making slow, delicious love to his chosen one. Yet, each time it had ended in disaster, with his lover dead, sucked dry by a vampire lost to his own carnal passions.

Though it still happened on occasion, he did not like to kill his victims, preferring instead to take as little as possible to slake his terrible thirst and then leave them be. Sex became an alternative—something to divert him from the blood-passion that spilled over his reason. He had learned not to mix the two when humans were involved.

With vampires, it was another thing altogether, and yet somehow such a connection had eluded him. In all his years wandering the globe, he had yet to meet a vampire who moved him with passion. Yes, he had taken his pleasure and even shared the sacred blood, but never, except with Adrienne had his spirit soared and looped with longing. Perhaps he was a romantic, holding out for his "true love". The desperate hope for connection had slowly faded, as he was forced by time to let go of the idea that he would somehow find his Adrienne.

Hurrying back, his hunger now sated for a while, Julian mused on the evening. A new lesson had been learned. These so-called blood bars were dangerous places. His own stark need had been revealed too clearly in front of the humans. He had grown careless this past decade, with these new groups of pretend vampires. He had allowed himself to be lulled into believing they wouldn't find his behaviors odd. Now he had gotten himself noticed, and the attention wasn't positive. He would collect Marguerite and leave quietly.

Quickly he returned to the little antique shop on Bourbon, licking a stray droplet of human blood from his lower lip. The old fellow greeted him with a smile and gestured toward the back of the dimly lit store. When Julian entered the dark little bar, he saw the group he had watched enter as he'd left.

They turned to look at him as he stepped into the place. Marguerite stood and called out, "Julian! There you are. What took you so long?" As Julian stepped further into the room, he saw something catch the light on the tall young man's neck. Looking closer for a moment, he did a double take. Too many coincidences tonight!

"Excuse me, sir," he said politely, his voice blandly hiding his inner excitement. "Where did you come upon such an interesting, ah, trinket?"

"Oh, this?" answered Robert, for that is who it was, with Rhonda and Mistress Margo in tow. His voice took on a didactic tone as if he were beginning a lecture. "This is called an amphora. Among the ancients, these vessels were used for holding sacred wine or special oils. They say that ancient vampires used the lip to cut their victim's throat just so." Robert unscrewed the little silver cap, revealing the bottle's sharp edge, holding it against his own neck.

"Is that so?" Julian willed away the sudden image of that diamond-sharp glass cutting the man's throat, allowing a gush of brilliant red. The fool was right in that vampires used these things, but wrong as to the purpose. Julian didn't correct him. "How did you come by it, if I may ask?"

"Oh. I bought it online. At a Coven Auction. I paid quite a bit for it, actually. I'm going to have copies of it made for members of my coven, the Red Covenant. It will be our symbol." He smiled proudly, as if waiting for congratulations.

Julian resisted a sudden impulse to rip the amphora from its delicate chain. Could this amphora be the very one used by the vampire Adrienne so long ago? If so, how had it left Adrienne's possession and ended up on an Internet auction site?

To possess such a thing! To imagine that it even existed. Taking a deep breath, he forced his features into a neutral, pleasant smile. He sensed that this man would enjoy withholding something another person wanted. He could feel the pettiness of the man's mind and his own instinct was immediate dislike. Yet, he could also feel the man's power. He was clearly a leader among men, or at least among those in his little group of playacting friends.

"Well, that truly is a lovely piece. Allow me to introduce myself. I am called Julian Gaston." Marguerite had sidled up near him and he nodded toward her adding, "And this is my companion for the evening, Marguerite."

"A pleasure," answered Robert, firmly shaking Julian's offered hand. "I am Robert. Robert Dalton. This is Mistress Margo, a sanguine vampire like myself, and my personal swan, Rhonda. Rhonda's going to donate tonight, aren't you, girl? If there is a taker, she is prepared to give her blood tonight. Are you, sir, a sanguine? Do you savor the taste of blood?"

Oh, if you only knew, you wretched human, Julian thought to himself. Then his eye caught Margo's. She was older than the others but still lovely. It wasn't her beauty that attracted him, at least not solely. Perhaps it was her expression, subtly ironic as she gazed at him. Probing her mind for a moment, he pulled back suddenly. On some level, perhaps not quite a conscious one, she knew what he was! They locked eyes for a moment, and Margo's lips curved up enigmatically.

"Julian's a real vampire!" Marguerite piped up excitedly, interrupting the silent communion between Julian and Margo. "He drinks blood! Lots of it. I bet he'd love to cut on Rhonda, wouldn't you, baby?"

What had he been thinking when he'd bedded this girl? The last vestige of desire slipped away as her words grated against his ears. Consciously avoiding Margo's eye, Julian smiled blandly and said, "Oh, occasionally I dabble in the blood-arts. But tonight I'm rather tired, I think. It's been wonderful meeting you all. Perhaps we could talk at a later date, Mr. Dalton, about that amphora. I would be interested in buying it from you. Perhaps we could discuss terms at a later date."

"Oh," Robert said, fingering the little bottle at his neck. Julian slipped into his thoughts, *I could make a fortune off this idiot. I could sell this for three times what I bought it. He looks like a sap. I'll do it.* Robert looked startled for a moment, as these thoughts bounced in his brain, confusing him. Then he smiled slightly, a greedy smile, and slipped a little card from his jacket. "My card, sir," he said pompously, as if he were a proper gentleman from the nineteenth century, instead of a twenty-something American boy who had never been out of Louisiana in all his short life.

Julian pocketed the card and left the little bar, determined to send Marguerite on her way with a few well-placed thoughts about what a tedious and boring man he himself was, and how much she would like to be rid of him.

* * * * *

Grace tried on several outfits before she decided on the teal-blue silk blouse over simple, black linen pants. The blouse set off the color of her hair nicely, she thought, as she eyed herself critically in the mirror. She would leave her hair down tonight, held in place only by a pearl barrette above each ear.

When Grace had last stumbled from that old mansion, shaken to the core, it was Margo's phone number that was clutched in her hand. At first, she'd only taken it at Margo's insistence. The whole experience had thoroughly shaken her up, and Grace's plan, her modus operandi most of her adult life, was to try to forget it had ever happened.

But this time she couldn't. The sweet peppery taste of blood now haunted her dreams each night. She would awaken in a sweat, crying out as the images of blood against white flesh tormented her. She found her appetite for food had diminished and yet her hunger for blood now raged, unabated and unsatisfied. Her sexual arousal had peaked as well and she couldn't keep her own fingers from her poor, hot little pussy. Even at work she found herself unable to concentrate, instead slipping off to the bathroom to hurriedly rub herself to some kind of meager relief. Though usually indifferent to the attentions of the men in her office, she suddenly found herself looking them over, trying to pick someone in her mind she would like to fuck. Alas, the selection was grim, mostly men twice her age or half her intellect. She had left work early on Thursday, feeling too weak and achy to concentrate.

When she had finally dared to dial Margo's number, the older woman's calm insistence that she come to the Red Covenant dinner that coming Saturday night had won her over. "You mustn't run anymore, Grace. There is something you need to confront. I know you're not ready yet, but don't shut yourself off from your own potential. Come to see me. Come to our dinner. We'll have a chance to talk then. And perhaps Rhonda will be your swan again."

"No!" Grace bit her lip. She would not subject herself to that uncontrollable display again. No! If they hadn't stopped her, how long would she have nursed at Rhonda's offered wound? And now the desire was so strong, she doubted she would let them stop her.

"Hush now, chérie," Margo had soothed, as if Grace had spoken aloud. "You don't have to do a thing you don't want to do. Just come and break bread with us, and meet some of the others. You are not alone in your bloodlust, dear. The more you learn the more you will be comforted, and the more you will learn to handle this gift."

"Gift?" This wretched pain in her gut? This pain and hunger that had been simmering just below the surface since she first entered puberty? What gift was this? Curse, it seemed to Grace. And so aloud, she said, "You mean this curse!"

"No, no," Margo answered. "Don't curse what you do not understand. There's a reason I want you to come. Robert has invited a man I think you should meet. Someone we met recently who took quite an interest in Robert's little amulet. His name is Julian Gaston and I believe that he is the real thing, my dear, just as I suspect you are."

The real thing. Grace didn't ask what she meant. She was right on the edge of her own understanding, but unwilling to hear it from another. Not yet.

Now here she was, dressing carefully in pretty silk to have dinner with a bunch of blood-fetishists at some creepy old mansion. Well, why not? This was New Orleans, after all, where anything could happen. And Margo wanted her to meet some dark mysterious stranger with a French name. Certainly, he'd be more interesting than Robert Dalton!

In the cool of the early evening, Grace picked her way past hidden courtyards and lacy balconies, past secret fountains splashing, leprous scaly stucco, monstrous greenery and live oaks dripping beards of moss, through surprising pockets of light where the air seemed to lie like colored veils. As she turned onto Charles Street, the familiar ache in her belly pulled at her, but something else was happening as well. A premonition. A feeling that something was going to happen. Something she had been waiting for, though she couldn't think what that might be.

She knocked upon the heavy old door and again it was Rhonda who opened it. "Oh, hello!" Rhonda said, smiling shyly. Grace smiled back uncertainly. Rhonda took her arm, gently pulling her into the room. "Grace, you were certainly something last Saturday! No one's ever done that to me. I can't stop thinking about it! Robert's actually jealous, can you believe it! He keeps cutting me, trying to do what you did, but it just isn't the same. He's a player, poor boy. I love him dearly, but he isn't the real thing. Not like you."

The real thing. Why did they all keep saying that? Grace forced herself to respond lightly, "Well, I don't know about that. It was an interesting experience, though. And I think you're very brave to do it."

"Oh, it isn't about bravery, silly. I get off on it. It gets me hot." When Grace glanced sharply at her, Rhonda blushed, high little spots of red against her pale freckled cheeks. She dropped Grace's arm and said more formally, "Come on. Most everyone's here."

Grace followed Rhonda into the large old-fashioned parlor. Her eyes lighted on Margo, sitting imperiously with her boy Mark kneeling at her feet, his head resting in her lap. Slowly she smoothed his lemon-colored head, the hair contrasting prettily with her wine-red velvet skirt.

"Grace," she called out, her voice rich and deep, "I'm so glad you could come." Robert appeared just then, coming to stand proprietarily behind Rhonda, dropping a long, thin hand on her shoulder.

"Thank you for inviting me," Grace said, feeling self-conscious. The heavy knocker sounded again on the door and Rhonda, with a little push from Robert, went to open it. Grace, still standing near the entrance hall, was wondering if she should go in and sit down when the door opened.

Sage and lemon balm. Sex. Desire. Lust. She was transported back for a moment to that day at the Vampire Ball, when that same delicious scent had assailed her nostrils, leaving her weak with desire. Turning, her eyes bright, her face flushed with expectation, Grace saw Rhonda ushering in an extremely handsome man, his features dark — dark eyes against fine white skin, dark hair like black silk cascading in smooth waves against his collarless linen shirt. Her eyes followed the curve of his strong chest tapering to a narrow waist. As she admired the well-muscled thighs encased in the softest toffee-brown leather, clearly tailored just for him, she couldn't help but notice the sexy bulge at his crotch.

But beyond the intense sexual attraction, there was something wildly and instantly compelling about this stranger. She felt her breath catch in her throat when he entered the room. When his eyes alighted upon hers, they seemed to be glinting with some secret laughter. *I have found you.* The thought tumbled into her brain, and though there was no sound, no timbre to the words, she somehow knew that this man had spoken them, though his lips had not moved and no sound issued from his red, luscious lips.

Suddenly Robert was looming, his lanky form insinuating itself between them. "Ah, Mr. Gaston. I am so pleased you were able to come." He fingered his amphora pointedly, his mind no doubt calculating the sums he would procure from this man.

"Thank you for your kind invitation, Mr. Dalton," Julian replied smoothly. His voice was deep and resonant, a continental accent just barely detectable which lent a roundness to his vowels and thoroughly charmed Grace. She stood rooted to the spot, leaning slightly to try and see his face as Robert continued to block her view.

Julian slipped to the side, his eyes burning into hers. "And who is this lovely lady?" he asked, making Grace's heart thump so hard in her chest that it actually hurt. Her pussy throbbed with need. What was happening to her?

"Ah," Robert said, "This is Grace. Grace Davis. She isn't part of our coven yet, but she definitely likes the taste of blood, don't you, Grace?" His smirk was irritating and Grace would have been annoyed but she didn't have time to focus on him. All of her attention was riveted on the sweet-smelling man whose eyes held hers in a lover's stare.

Slowly she held out her hand and Robert seemed to disappear, fading into insignificance. "I'm Grace," she whispered.

"Julian," he smiled, taking her hand in his. *I've been waiting for you.*

If asked afterwards, Grace couldn't remember what they had for dinner, or what the conversation was. From the moment his hand touched hers, something seemed to switch on inside of her. She felt heightened somehow, more alive. It was as if she had been passing through her life in a kind of dream state, only half aware of her surroundings and suddenly she had opened her eyes.

As far as she knew, she sat through the dinner, directly across from the mysterious man, behaving like a normal person, eating, drinking and nodding when people said something to her. But all she saw was his face, the eyes dark and focused solely on hers. She saw herself in the mirror of his eyes, heard his voice whisper inside her head.

They didn't touch. When they spoke it was of nothing, nothing she could recall. Though they sat apart, their inner selves seemed to almost rise up and meet while their bodies remained seated.

The gnawing in her gut sharpened. When the diners adjourned to the living room for a cutting demonstration, she had a sudden vivid image of leaping toward Mark, the chosen donor of the evening and sinking her teeth into his neck. She could almost taste the precious, bright blood.

She must have stood up from her seat because suddenly Grace felt a hand on her arm.

His hand.

His fingers were long and blunt-tipped as they wrapped gently around her bare forearm. Inside her head she heard, *Sit down, Grace. He is not for you. I am for you. I know what you are. I have found you at last.*

She turned toward him sharply, but Julian was not looking at her. In fact, he had stood and was now saying to the company at large, "If you will forgive us, Grace and I have another engagement. We must go now."

All eyes turned to them in surprise, except perhaps Mistress Margo, who simply smiled a small smile, nodding her head imperceptibly.

"But," sputtered Robert, "You can't go yet! The fun is just beginning! Anyway, you don't even *know* her. *I* introduced you! And the amphora—" he fingered the trinket. "You wanted to buy this! I don't usually sell my Objects d'Art, but I might be persuaded."

"Another time perhaps, Mr. Dalton," Julian said.

Careful Grace, shy Grace, left the old mansion without a backward glance, Julian Gaston's hand delicately resting on her elbow as he guided her away.

They walked quietly for a while and Grace realized they were moving toward her little apartment. Did he know where she lived? Who was this man? This perfect man whom she had always known? Julian spoke, his voice gentle, the underlying urgency barely detectable. "I know what you are, Grace. But do you know? I've been able to enter your mind, but have felt only the barest hint of telepathy from you. I smell the scent of our kind on you and yet, I don't see the mark of knowledge in your eyes."

Grace turned toward him, her knee-jerk reaction to question, to deny, to refuse. But the words died on her lips as he bent toward her. Slowly they kissed, an exploration of each other's lips and mouths. His strong arms encircled her body as he bent her back, kissing her harder now, his tongue probing, forcing her lips apart. When at last they pulled apart, it was Grace who leaned forward, her mouth open, her eyes glittering with lust.

"Who are you?" she managed to whisper. Her heart was thudding against her bones, the blood roaring in her ears.

"You know who I am. It is time you accept your fate. I am a vampire, as are you, Grace. One of the true kin, the sacred circle."

Chapter Eight

Grace felt breathless as if she couldn't properly fill her lungs. The humid New Orleans night air hung heavy against her. The sidewalk seemed to loom and tilt in front of her and a bile rose in her throat. "Please," she murmured, barely able to hear herself over the ringing in her ears. "I think I'm going to be sick."

Mercifully, they were passing a little park and Julian was able to steer Grace toward a low, wrought iron bench. Grace sank gratefully down, dropping her head into her hands. Gently, Julian pulled her hair back from her face. Her forehead was damp with sweat.

"Calm yourself, my lady. Breathe slowly. I can see this is a shock. I've seen it before though not for many years. It is rare that a vampire comes to be without being aware of the circumstances of their existence. What of your parents?"

"I'm adopted," Grace answered faintly. "But there's no such thing as vampires. Only in folklore. Maybe long ago. Not today. Those people just playact. It's all a game."

Julian took Grace's face in his hand, two fingers on her chin forcing her to meet his eyes. "Listen to me, Grace. I see the mark of the true kin on you. I smell the scent. I can also see that you haven't yet had the knowledge shared. Though you have tasted the blood, haven't you? I saw the bloodlust shining in your eyes tonight. You have tasted the sweet nectar and you know what it is to hunger."

Grace shook her head, pulling away from Julian's touch. "No! How could it be! If I were a vampire, if there were such a thing, wouldn't I have needed the blood to survive? I'm twenty-four, for God's sake! How could I have gone this long without human blood?"

"How indeed?" Julian mused, his mind scanning back twenty-four years to any mention of a birth. Nothing sparked in his mind. "It is unusual, but not unheard of. Untrained and untutored, a vampire's blood-thirst can remain dormant well into puberty. Did you have no desire? No pain in your belly, a gnawing need in your gut? Are you sensitive to light, preferring the dusk to the blazing noonday sun? Oh, the myths that vampires can't tolerate sunlight are highly exaggerated, but there is a germ of truth. We prefer the softer light of the moon." He touched her pale cheek, his expression knowing as he continued, "Have you a fascination with blood, with its sweet red possibilities? An interest in the history and legends of our kind?"

As Grace stared at him, her eyes wide, he continued, "And when you tasted the blood, did it overwhelm you? Its taste was surely sweeter than the finest wine, and far more powerful. How often have you had the blood, Grace? Do you long for it now?"

Grace began to cry, jerky little sobs generated by fear and confusion. "Please! I don't know what's happening. How do you know all this about me! How are you getting inside my head! What's going on?" She hid her face again in her hands, the tears slipping between her fingers as she cried.

Julian smoothed her head and wrapped his strong arm around her heaving shoulders. He didn't try to speak or address her many questions. He sent gentle soothing thoughts into her mind and waited patiently. The time for explanations could wait a little longer.

At length, her tears subsided and she accepted the large white handkerchief Julian had produced from his pocket. "I'm sorry," she said, smiling weakly. "I don't usually sob on a first date."

Julian smiled broadly and said, "You have a lot to take in. I know it must be very confusing and difficult for you. But I assure you, this is no game we are playing and I am no actor. Let's go get a coffee and some beignets, and I'll try to answer the many questions you must have. I have some as well."

"We could go to my apartment. It's just a few blocks from here." The sudden image in her mind of Julian naked and beautiful in her bed made Grace shiver with a barely controlled desire. She turned her face away, afraid her feelings were revealed.

"No. I'm sorry, but no." Julian touched her arm, and Grace started a little as if he had jolted her with electricity. "You feel it, too, I know. There is a connection between us that goes beyond mere vampire kindredness. We are meant to be lovers." Grace blushed as he continued, "I haven't lain with another vampire for many years. You aren't ready. Not yet. Trust me, Grace. Not yet."

"Well, I wasn't inviting you to bed!" Grace's blush darkened, her normally pale cheeks pink with embarrassment. This man was dangerous! He could read her thoughts as if she were shouting them! She tossed her hair, standing up from the bench. Yet, her pussy had responded warmly to his remarks about them becoming lovers and lying together. She felt her nipples tingling and had to resist an impulse to rub and pull on them through the thin silk of her blouse.

Glancing sidelong at the mysterious man standing next to her, she suddenly worried that he really could read her mind, but he was grinning at her, seeming to respond only to her words, not her body's desires. "No, of course not," he nodded. "It is I who would lack the self-control. I have been waiting for three hundred years for the possibility of you. I can wait a little longer."

"Three hundred years! You really expect me to believe that!"

"I expect nothing. I don't demand your understanding or even acceptance. Though I am willing to explain. You are owed at least that. But there is time, all the time in the world. For now, let's have our coffee."

They found a little café and were soon sipping café au lait and pulling apart fresh beignets. For once, Grace found her appetite as she bit into the hot fried dough sprinkled liberally with powdered sugar, a bit of which found its way to the tip of her nose. The dark-roasted coffee and chicory served with sugar and hot milk was the perfect drink for this particular dessert. Julian, who hadn't touched the donuts, sipped his coffee thoughtfully as he watched the young woman eat.

She looked up at him and grinned self-consciously as she wiped her face with the large cloth napkin. "I didn't realize I was hungry," she said. "I don't usually have an appetite."

"No, of course you don't," Julian nodded. "Why do you think that is, Grace?" As she looked away, he let the matter drop. Keeping his voice deliberately casual he asked, "So, you were adopted? Do you know who your birth parents were?"

"No. They found me. I was abandoned in a basket on the stairs of the Cathedral of St. Louis in Jackson Square! Like something out of a fairytale, don't you think? As a child, I always found it terribly romantic, though as I got older, I often wondered what kind of parents would do such a thing? What kind of mother."

"A desperate one, perhaps. One who didn't want to or couldn't afford to be identified?" Julian pursed his lips, leaning his chin against the steeple of his fingers. "Vampire babies are rare. Usually their arrival is well marked in our scattered but connected society. I don't recall a baby twenty-four years ago." He stared into space, his eyes narrowed in concentration.

"I didn't think vampires could procreate! I mean, I guess they had to start somewhere, but it's not really discussed in the literature."

"The literature, huh? You are well-read, then, on these vampires whose existence you claim to deny?"

Grace flushed and ducked her head, "Well, I...uh...that is, it's just a passing curiosity, naturally."

"Naturally." His smile was sardonic. "At any rate, yes, we do procreate, but rarely. Vampires are even more tied to the cycles of the moon than humans. The situation must be very precise for a female vampire to conceive. A blue moon is necessary, which as you may know only occurs about forty times a century. Then, of course, vampires rarely couple. The experience is quite intense and most vampires seek out humans for sexual interaction. I myself have only laid with a female vampire a handful of times."

Grace was staring at him. "This is real, isn't it? I want to disbelieve you. I keep telling myself you're just a better actor than the others, but I know that's not true. Something in my bones tells me you are what you say you are. And yet, how can it be? Life isn't like that! There are no vampires! It's just fantasy and an overactive imagination."

"Oh, is it? And my ability to enter your mind is not real? And the gnawing in your gut? The bloodlust in your eyes, which marks you as clearly as if you were wearing a sign?" As Grace gasped, Julian continued relentlessly, "And my scent, which you no doubt smelled when you first encountered me, as I could discern yours, though humans cannot smell it. They haven't the capacity. You needn't admit it—I already know it.

"But I am curious, more than curious," he went on, "as to who it was who abandoned you, and why. Perhaps you and I were meant to meet. I don't believe in coincidence. Perhaps I am destined not only to be your lover, but your guide. Perhaps an adventure awaits us!"

Grace didn't know what to focus on. He was offering too much, too fast. Seizing on one facet, still trying to maintain her skepticism, she demanded, "How come I've been able to stay alive until now with only a few tastes of the blood? From all my research—" she flushed slightly, now admitting tacitly that hers was more than a passing interest, " —vampires need human blood to survive. It isn't merely a pleasure or a compulsion, it's a necessity."

"Well, that's true, actually. But as I mentioned, some vampires remain dormant. It's almost like you're in a suspended state until you first taste the blood. And even then, if you don't drink sufficiently, it can remain in a mostly dormant state. Though you pay the price in pain and in longing."

He looked at her keenly. "Tell me honestly, when did you first taste human blood? And how did you feel afterwards? It must have been a terrible and confusing burden for you. To feel the need but not understand the reason." His voice was compassionate and Grace felt hot tears again prick her eyelids.

She answered, haltingly at first, telling him honestly about her early experiences with her own blood, with the cutting and the therapy and her own hot denial. Hesitantly, and then with more courage she continued, almost stumbling over her words as she described the recent experience with Rhonda and how she couldn't stop her feeding.

"My God," she said now, her eyes huge with fear and wonder. "I do believe I would have sucked the very life out of her if they hadn't stopped me, Julian."

"I believe you would have, Grace. I'm impressed that you were able to stop, and to behave with such grace." He smiled, and she smiled back at the play on her name.

"But how could I have gone all these years? Assuming we accept your explanation of dormancy until puberty, I did in fact taste blood and yet managed to go another ten years without it! Only in my dreams." She stopped abruptly and turned away. The dark-haired man in her dreams! Julian! The sweet, cruel lover of her fevered dreams sharing the blood. The blood!

"I feel your confusion, Grace. Your excitement. Your passions. Please, let yourself go. The time is finally past for censuring and controlling your thoughts and your dreams. Your needs. That constant pain in your belly, it's there, isn't it? Even now, a dull ache you've come to accept as part of who you are."

"Yes, yes!" Grace whispered, unaware that tears were rolling down her cheeks. Slowly she leaned forward, her lips parting for his. Their fingers locked together as their lips met in a delicate kiss. Like a slow fuse, their passion burned down, igniting as their tongues met again.

They left the little café, walking slowly in no particular direction. Eventually they arrived at Grace's apartment house. The familiar magnolia still heavy with summer blossoms dropped its branches protectively over them. She was half-relieved, half-disappointed when he again refused her invitation to come into her apartment.

"It's late and you've been through some pretty amazing stuff tonight, Grace. If I come in there, I'm afraid there'll be no turning back. Let's go just a little slowly. Give you a chance to absorb the shock of all this revelation."

Gently he kissed her again, this time without a lover's passion. Smoothing back her hair, he said, "I'm staying at the Worthington, the penthouse suite. I'll be there waiting when you're ready to see me. I promise I'm not going anywhere. For now, get some rest. When you're ready, call me and I'll come to you." He stroked her thin cheek, adding, "I think our first order of business is to get some flesh on these bones. You need to feed properly. I will take you and teach you the ways of our people. I will teach you to hunt, Grace."

Instinctively, Grace's mouth filled with saliva and she swallowed, the promise of blood hot in her brain. Yet he was right, she felt almost overcome with fatigue. There was so much to process and absorb. Now that she stood on the brink of some kind of salvation, she found herself almost hesitating. It was as if she might reach out for an illusion that would shatter her as it slipped from her grasp.

Looking up into Julian's dark eyes, she searched for another offering of proof.

She felt his thoughts, heard his words whispering sweet and warm against her mind. *It will come with time, dear girl. Your trust will spring from experience. I will prove myself worthy of you, as you will learn with me. For now, just sleep. Take your new knowledge to your heart and rejoice in our discovery. Your life is finally beginning.*

Chapter Nine

"He's a good choice, I think. That one there, with the crack pipe." Julian and Grace were standing on a dark corner in a seedy part of town—both dressed in black T-shirts and black jeans, barely discernable against the night. No tourists came this way. There were no jazz bars, no little bistros, no bright lights or river walks strung with softly glowing lanterns swaying in the moist tropical breeze. No, this was the part of New Orleans the tourists never saw, but Julian knew it well.

As always, as he ventured into these crime-ridden, drug-infested neighborhoods that sprawled just outside the garish lights of the French Quarter, Julian was struck by the glaring disparity of rich and poor in this wonderful, terrible town. And it had been always thus, he mused, since its early days as a backwater swamp, where riches were piled on the backs of slaves.

Grace jolted him back to the present. "Julian, I don't think I'm ready. Please."

"No one is ready their first time. I will help you. I'll be here. It is time you had the blood. Properly, not just a sip."

Grace shivered. Though the night was warm, she felt the goose bumps rise on her arms, and she clutched herself protectively. She wanted what he offered. God, did she want it. Yet, she was terrified. Terrified of the act itself, and perhaps even more so of her own reaction.

It was one thing to have an academic discussion about her "true nature". It was quite another to be crouching in an alleyway, watching a gaunt man in filthy clothes sucking on a little clay pipe, his head nodding into his chest between puffs. Though the man himself repelled her, the thought of his sweet red blood bursting against her teeth made her almost faint with desire. She recognized that her desire was not only physical but sexual. Her pussy throbbed gently at the prospect of piercing that man's flesh with her perfect canines. At the same time, she felt shame that she seemed to care so little about the man himself. Her need was too great.

Julian had explained that he sought his victims carefully. He tried to choose people who were already close to the edge of life, one foot dangling over the abyss. Usually addicts like this one, or drunks, without homes who lived on the fringe of society, courting death as if it were a lover. And even so, he tried not to kill them. He had learned to curb himself, even in the throes of his feeding ecstasy, before he went too far. Though sometimes, his greed overcame his reason and someone died as a result.

"Have you killed someone, then? Been unable to stop before it was too late?" Grace held her breath, already certain of his answer.

"Yes, yes I have. Many times, though never with intent. But many more times I have not. It is the way of the true kin, Grace. Most vampires don't give it a second thought. But I value life, even human life, and try to spare it when I can. Tonight we will not kill. I will keep you safe. Now come, let us ease the pain in your body, let us feed your soul."

So they crept closer, her thirst now overpowering her fear. The man was already barely conscious—an easy mark for Julian to get behind and lock into a chokehold that soon rendered him inert, lost in cocaine-laden dreams. Though he rarely bothered for himself, Julian had thoughtfully brought along a wet handkerchief, which he now rubbed across the man's bared throat, paying special attention to the jugular poking up like a serpent under the sallow, dirty skin.

Grace was trembling now, her body shaking as she knelt down next to the pair in the dark. "I don't know how," she whispered.

"You do. It's your instinct. It's as natural as a babe suckling its mother's breast. Here." He positioned the man easily across his lap, baring the neck for her bite. "Sit next to me. That's it. Now lean over and just sink your teeth in. You'll see. The skin will yield to you like a ripe peach. You were born to this, Grace. This is your destiny, your right. Take what is yours for the first time. Take it. Do it."

She did. Leaning over, her golden-red hair spilling around her face, she bit down. Her teeth sank easily, as he had promised. There was no tearing of jagged flesh, no ripping of tendon or muscle. She connected easily with the vein, feeling a little rubbery resistance for a moment, which yielded suddenly and sweetly in a steady flow of pure heaven. Without being aware she was doing it, Grace wrapped her arms around the man, pulling him up in a lover's hold.

Grace forgot Julian in that moment. She forgot the years of confusion and denial. She forgot the painful longing for something she didn't understand. It was as if her whole life had tilted toward this moment. For the very first time, she felt comfortable in her own skin. She felt whole and alive! The blood pulsed in the man's throat, throbbing sweetly against her mouth. Oh, it was heaven. It was everything. There was nothing but this. She gulped, trying to take it all, never wanting it to stop.

Something like rage assailed her when Julian pulled her from her lover's kiss. "Enough. I said enough!" Dimly she became aware that he was talking. That he had in fact been talking for some minutes, entreating her to stop before it was too late. Now he had forcibly separated her from the only thing she wanted in this world — sweet, perfect, rich red blood.

She fought him, flailing her arms and seeking that sweetmeat again with her mouth opened like a little bird's. "I must! You don't understand! I must."

"I understand all too well. And if you persist, you will kill him. Already I let you go too far. He may not survive this night as it is. Another of your kisses will be fatal, Grace. Do you want to kill your first time out? Do you want the death of a human on your hands so soon?" The horror of his words finally penetrated her bloodlust, and Grace went limp in his grip.

"What have I done?" she whispered faintly, slumping now against him. Carefully, Julian lowered her to the ground and then focused on the unconscious man, touching briefly the two tiny holes at the side of his neck. A vampire's mark was hard to discern and usually the bite completely healed within a few days. Grace had drunk deeply and Julian secretly doubted if this man, already weak to begin with, would recover.

Such was the risk and the burden of their lot. He would spare Grace this night, however, and he said now, "Come, Grace. He's fine. He will awaken in the morning no more the worse for wear. He's killing himself so quickly with crack that he probably won't survive the month." He handed her a cloth to wipe the red smears of human blood from her mouth and chin.

They walked slowly back to the main road. Traces of blood from their prey were effectively hidden against the black fabric of their clothing. Soon they found themselves back among the bright lights and hubbub of the French Quarter. Grace, now assured of the man's recovery, had a queer light in her eyes. They were over-bright, as if with fever and she was talking very rapidly. Julian let her go on, remembering his own euphoria after his first real drink.

"The pain, Julian! My God! It's gone. For the first time that I can remember, I'm not in pain! I feel so alive! So full of energy! I could lift a house! I could move a mountain! I could fly!" Running ahead of him, she turned back, twirling in her delight. Her laughter was like a cascade, tripping down a musical scale of pure glee. People passing smiled indulgently. Another drunk tourist making merry. There were hundreds like her every day of the week.

The sky was lightening, streaks of pink and gold spilling into the velvet indigo, sucking away the color. "Why aren't I tired, Julian? It's dawn and I feel as if I could run a race! Rule the world!"

Julian smiled, "It's your first time. It's not unlike your first sexual experience except that in your case, this was really a life-giving elixir. You've literally been starving yourself to death. You are like a desert flower, the kind that lie dormant for years before the torrential rains finally come and you bloom in all your splendid beauty. You are only just claiming your true heritage, my love. Who would want to sleep at a time like that!"

Grace nodded, thinking back to two days before, when he had left her at her door. Then she had slept, falling heavily onto her bed still fully clothed. She hadn't been prepared for the utter fatigue that had dropped over her like a net once he'd left her. The sheer mental weight of the astounding revelations had left her weak and exhausted, so much so that she wasn't yet able to savor the little bud of excitement, of potential, flowering within her.

Julian had been right to leave her alone and she had slept deeply, not noticing the hot sun rising steadily in the steamy heat or falling again into a golden, purple haze. When she had awoken at last, it was the old gnawing in her gut that interrupted dreamless sleep. Her mind roused more slowly, images of the handsome strange man mixing with the promise of blood. She, a vampire! Her parents, her *real* parents, must have been of the true kin, as he called them. The true kin, the sacred circle. She liked the ring of the words. She felt contented suddenly. Even though the mystery of her parentage was still a dark tangle, she was one of them. Grace, who had never fit in, was suddenly part of something, something sacred and infinite, a circle with no beginning and no end. For the first time, she felt she belonged somewhere.

Eventually she sat up and saw to her surprise that she must have slept the day away! Julian was waiting for her at his penthouse suite. How glamorous it all sounded. Would she call him today or wait a while longer? She got up slowly, stretching her long, thin limbs and shaking out her thick hair. Pulling off her old wrinkled things, she walked naked to her bathroom and started the shower, which quickly filled the little room with steam.

As she soaped her body, her hands cupped her breasts, gently pulling the little nipples erect as she thought of Julian. A hand slid down to her silky pussy and she sighed. No, she wouldn't wait any longer. There was no point in pretending to either of them that anything was left to consider. She would call him just as soon as she was out of the shower. And that is precisely what she had done.

Now as the dawn crept over her sill, they sat together in her small living room, with Grace making laughing apologies about the state of her household. Books were piled on the coffee table in front of the low-slung modern couch and a stack of magazines was on the floor next to it. Bookshelves lined the walls, crammed with scholarly tomes mixed in among well-thumbed paperbacks. The place was clean but definitely cluttered.

"This is the home of someone who spends a lot of time alone," Julian remarked. Grace flushed slightly but nodded. "Please, sit down. I'll bring you something to drink." She gestured toward the couch, and Julian sank down gracefully. Grace's mouth felt dry, and she realized she was nervous, not certain what to expect now that they were at last alone in her apartment.

Still standing she answered, "It's true. I've never had a lot of friends. Even my friend Regan — I mean, she's good for a few laughs or diversion, but I've never been able to connect with anyone. Not in a meaningful way. I mean — " she flushed a little as she realized what she was about to admit but decided to plunge on, " — I've been with lots of guys but it never really meant anything, you know? It was almost like I was scratching an itch when really it was something so much deeper I was searching for. I've even had two serious relationships, but in the end it was only about the sex. Maybe in the beginning, too." She grinned but then continued more seriously. "I like sex. Sometimes it's almost like a distraction. I mean, from the pain." She stopped, her eyes pleading for understanding.

Julian continued her thought for her. "The pain of longing. Because you have never, until tonight, been fulfilled. Never had the blood your body has craved. And so you used sex as a way to try and deflect that pain. To ease it for just that moment in time."

"You do understand," Grace breathed.

"Of course. I do the same thing. Though I have recourse, because I understood what I was, while you, my poor darling, have had to suffer alone without understanding. How brave you are!"

Grace looked embarrassed but pleased. She said, "I don't feel brave. I mean, I always just felt strange. Lonely. People say I'm aloof, standoffish. I don't mean to be."

"Please," Julian interrupted, "You needn't explain to *me*. A vampire's life is usually a lonely one. It was especially hard for you, not knowing the cause. Knowing you were different but not knowing why or how."

"Stop," Grace pleaded. "You're going to make me cry again, and I don't want to cry! I feel so happy! For the first time, Julian. Truly happy." She sat next to him, though not close enough to touch. He leaned toward her, his strong thigh touching hers. Grace moved away abruptly, and said a little too brightly, "That drink! I promised you a drink. What would you like? A bit of white wine, perhaps? Or since it's practically morning, some orange juice?"

Julian touched Grace's arm and said, "Nothing, Grace. I don't want a drink. Not of your wine or juice, at any rate. Relax. Sit here a moment next to me. You've had a long night, my dear." Grace sat back, though her back was rigid, her thighs pressed together.

Julian touched her arm softly. She felt so fragile. He could break her if he wished. He could take her by force and plunder that sweet softness. Bite into perfect flesh as he fucked her. A double rape. Delicious and all encompassing. Of course, he could do that. But of course, he would not.

It had been so long since he'd found another of the true kin, and one with whom he felt such an instant and deep rapport. He could see that she was frightened. That she wanted to trust him but didn't yet, not fully. So much had happened in so short a time. Like a schoolboy he had stayed in his rooms, willing the telephone to ring, resisting his own impulse to go back to her, to break the useless little locks on her door and take what was his.

But he knew patience, even if he didn't like it. Let her sleep, what was another day, another week? He realized that he was refusing to even entertain the notion that she wouldn't call. That she would refuse what he offered, deny what she was. No, he had felt her desire, her longing for connection on so many levels, even though she wasn't yet ready to accept it. There was so much more to gain by giving her the time she needed to come to it on her own.

And when that call had come—really only fourteen hours after he had first left her, how his silly heart had soared! He'd had to laugh at himself, recalling that fresh love made one stupid. How long had it been since he'd permitted himself the indignity of longing? Ah, but this wasn't about permission and he knew it. She had wrapped herself around his heart the minute that door on Charles Street had been opened and he'd seen her face, shining with uncertain and desperate recognition.

He looked at her now, tenderly touching her hand. Had he been wise to give her that first taste of blood so soon? Yes, it was clear she was wasting away. An adult vampire who had never properly slaked her blood-thirst. He must feed her regularly now, and teach her to catch her own prey. In some ways, Grace was like a child. His foundling, just learning the mysteries of her birthright. But as he gazed now at the tempting curve of her high, round breast against the soft cotton of her T-shirt he admitted to himself that she was no child. She was a woman. A woman of his own kind.

Julian licked his lips and shifted a little on the couch. He could feel his erection press its way against his leg, begging for attention. He put his arm around the girl, letting his hand drop so that his fingers grazed the hollow at her collarbone. Grace shivered a little and leaned sweetly against him.

"You smell so *good!*" she sighed. And then, as if remembering something, "Say, you were there, weren't you? At the Vampire Coven Ball, a couple of weeks back! I smelled your scent, but I didn't know what I was smelling. I only knew I wanted to find the source."

"I was, indeed. And I sensed you as well. But when I went in search of you, you had disappeared."

Grace sighed. "Oh, yes, that's me. I rarely stay for anything. Party pooper extraordinaire," she laughed ruefully.

"Well, you stayed long enough to get an invitation from that pompous, silly fellow, Robert. So whatever you did, fate intervened and here we are."

"Yes, here we are." She spoke lightly, though Julian felt her nervousness. Yet underneath it was her desire. He could feel that she was aroused by his scent, by his proximity, by his very being. And he found her beautiful.

Even if she had not been a vampire, he admired her thick, lustrous red and gold hair, her fair silky skin, her clear blue-green eyes. She was tall and slender, too thin but he would help her heal, now that she had admitted to her true nature. Her skin was so pale, another mark of a vampire. Though vampires soaked themselves in human blood, it barely seemed to suffuse the skin, instead being absorbed as a life force within.

He leaned down, this time moving in to her until their lips met. He kissed her slowly, his tongue twirling against her soft lips, moving past them to her hot, wet, little mouth. He had wanted to go slowly, had meant to. Oh, but the entire evening and night of restraint! Of watching her take the blood but taking none himself, though his mouth had salivated while he watched, and his cock had pulsed with suppressed need. Of being so close to one of the true kin, one whom he could claim with a look if he wished. And yet, he had waited all these hours, because he knew she needed at least a little time to absorb so much.

Her whole life had been altered when he'd entered that old mansion on Charles Street. And surely his as well. Grabbing a handful of rich, thick hair, Julian bent Grace's head back so he could kiss her more fully. She was trapped beneath him, her firm breasts mashing against his hard chest as he pulled her to him. He could feel her nipples harden and press against him, and his own cock snaked along his leg, painfully constrained in the soft denim of his pants.

"Jesus, I have to have you, Grace. I can't wait another moment."

Grace moaned and tried to protest, but her cries were lost in his kisses. "I know you're afraid, my love. You have a right to be. But know you can trust me. I will not harm you. I will not give you more than you can receive, though it might feel that way at first. Trust me. I have chosen you."

He stood, sweeping the young woman easily up into his arms. Her little sandals fell from her feet and he kicked them aside. His mouth found hers again, and they kissed passionately for another moment. Still carrying her, he walked back toward her little bedroom. He stood her next to her bed and commanded, "Take off those clothes. I must see you."

Grace, her face flushed, her eyes bright with need, still hesitated. It was ironic, as she'd admitted freely to lying with many men before Julian, using them to ease her vampire longings. Yet, Julian knew, sensing it in her mind, that she was shy now precisely because this was *not* like all the other times. Tonight mattered. Tonight wasn't just about sex as release or as a mask for other needs.

Tonight was about the potential for something new, something that mattered. Tonight was about love.

As Grace stood, wrapping her arms protectively around her thin torso, Julian smiled, the curve of his lips almost cruel. Dominant by nature, he was perversely aroused by her shyness. He would *take* what he wanted, whether or not she was willing to give it.

"I said strip, girl! Don't just stand there like a virgin. You know you want it. You know I can see into your heart and your mind, and I know your true desires. You want me as you have never craved another person. This coyness is not necessary, my love. We know what we are and what we want."

Grace blushed, but slowly began to obey, lifting the black shirt from her body, pulling it free over her head.

Her breasts, high and proud, were barely covered by the little lace demi-bra she wore. Her ribs were etched just below the skin of her narrow torso. Her eyes on his, she unzipped her jeans and stepped out of them, kicking them aside. Again, she wrapped her arms about herself, looking very young and vulnerable before her potential lover.

"Drop your arms. I want to see your beauty." His dark eyes locked on hers, and the spell he could cast so easily on human women worked on Grace as well. Slowly she dropped her slender arms to her sides. He could see the pulse of her pounding heart throbbing gently at her throat. He bit his own lower lip to keep from seizing her then and there. While he wanted her desperately, he didn't want to rape her. He wanted her to want it as much as he did.

Quickly, he stripped off his own T-shirt, tossing it aside. He kicked off his sneakers as he stared at her with burning eyes. At the same time, he unbuttoned his jeans, the bulge of his cock clearly evident beneath. He saw her little pink tongue darting quickly over her lips. Her nipples were pale pink and distended against the silky fabric of her brassiere. As shy as she might be tonight, her desire for him was clear.

Her waist was long and narrow but the hips flared out in a womanly way. Her pelvic bones created a little hollow between themselves across which stretched her little lace panties. Julian moved close so that their bodies were almost touching. He slipped a strong hand into that little hollow, cupping her dark-auburn pubic curls. His fingers slipped between her legs, feeling the delicate labia of her sex. Grace gasped and stepped back, but Julian wrapped his other arm around her, forcing her to remain in front of him.

"You need this, Grace. You were born for me." His voice was deep and soft as his fingers probed her hot pussy, pulling the moisture from her. Ah, she was wet but so tight! Like a little virgin, though she had said she'd been with many men before him.

In this era where virginity was no longer valued, there was still something to be said for it. For the delicious terror mixed with lust in a young girl's eyes when you first pressed the head of your hard cock against her tight, little entrance. For the impossibly tight grip of muscles just learning their use, made tighter still by inexperience and fear. Julian thrust a finger into Grace's cunt, and watched with pleasure and delight, as that same fear and arousal made itself plain on her face. And yet, she didn't pull back, even when he loosened his grip on her shoulder.

The girl was a virgin in spirit! That much was clear. Julian's penis was thrust up against his belly, fully erect. The smell of Grace's desire wafted sweetly up to him, making him groan with lust.

Quickly he released his member from its denim and silk prison, pulling the underwear down along with the pants, which he kicked aside, already forgotten as he focused on the beautiful, trembling woman before him.

"Grace, are you ready to submit to me?" Slowly she nodded, her eyes wide, the clear marine blue of an ocean. "Yes, I can see you are." His eyes held hers as he silently entered her mind, giving her a direct order. She proceeded to obey, unhooking the clasps that held her breasts encased in lace. Still keeping her eyes on his, she bent slightly, drawing her panties down her lean thighs, past her slender ankles as she stepped lightly out of them.

She stood, no longer blushing but proud and straight as he approached her. She was firmly in his trance, but it was not only his doing. She wanted to be there, and now she leaned into him, wrapping her arms around him as he pressed his iron rod against her belly.

And even though she did want him, still her body was trembling. Slowly he lowered her to the bed, his hands gently pressing her shoulders until she lay on her back, her legs still over the edge of the bed, bare feet almost touching the floor. He knelt between her legs, pushing them apart with his body. For a moment, Grace resisted him, trying to close her thighs but he was too strong for her.

Then his tongue found the sweet folds below her dark-auburn triangle and she shuddered. His large hands were on either thigh, holding her open as he sent jolts of shivery pleasure coursing through her body. She tasted of heaven and he longed to pierce the flesh with his perfect teeth. He knew she wasn't ready for that. Yet, the need was pulsing in his veins, making him moan with it as she, too, moaned in her pleasure.

He had only planned to make human love to her. She wasn't ready to share the sacred blood of the true kin. She needed to get stronger first. But as Grace began to buck and surge against his mouth, Julian felt the pulse of his desire pounding in his brain. Lovely girl, so sexy as she orgasmed with shuddery sighs against him.

He had only meant to kiss her thigh, but his teeth were suddenly bared, the canine fangs now discernibly longer than a human's as they plunged into tender flesh. Grace, still caught in the throes of her orgasm, barely registered the sharp pricks of his teeth against her. He sucked at her thigh, the sweet, heady blood bubbling up against his tongue. When had blood tasted so sweet? Not for close to three hundred years. Only a mouthful, then just one more!

Julian forced himself to stop. Indeed, he wanted to stop because he wanted to mount her. To claim her in the most primal of ways. To seduce her into wanton submission, firmly under his control. Now he rose over her, his huge cock bobbing at her lips as he knelt over the girl. "Take it," he said softly, and Grace's eyes flew open. She gasped at the size of his member. It was hard as a rock, but its skin was satin-soft. Carefully she licked the large head, her pink tongue slipping around it, making him almost beg.

But Julian didn't beg—he commanded. Kneeling up, he pressed his erection against her lips, forcing them to part as he slowly slid into her mouth. Grace stayed very still—her eyes closed now, her body inert beneath his. Her mouth felt hot and sweet against his flesh. He felt her teeth lightly grazing his cock as he slid it further back into her throat. Her lips closed upon him and he groaned with pleasure, as she seemed to come alive, gripping him with lips, tongue and teeth.

Julian was out of control as Grace gently cupped his heavy balls with long, cool fingers while she continued to suckle and tease his cock. Oh, it was too perfect! Julian pulled back suddenly, while Grace still held his penis with her lips and teeth. Those sharp teeth pulled across his flesh and Julian gasped as Grace's eyes glittered with bloodlust.

For the second time she consciously used her fledgling telepathic skills, sending these words to the strong man leaning over her. *I want your blood. I want the blood of the true kin. Don't deny me what I was born for. I'm ready. Take me, Julian. All I ask in return is your life.*

"Mon Dieu!" Julian breathed, for a moment forgetting his English, reverting to the tongue of his youth. He lay across the naked girl, pulling her up with him properly onto the bed. "You don't know what you ask, my love. Sharing the blood between lovers is a risky business. You haven't yet the strength."

She answered, "You already took *my* blood with your kisses. I felt it. I felt the sting and somehow it only heightened the pleasure of your mouth against me."

"Grace, you are wise beyond your tender years. You will find in our journey together that pain and pleasure are not always distinguishable. I consider them to be alternate extremes of a circular spectrum, best enjoyed together."

"Please. Make love to me, Julian. Don't make me wait any longer. I feel as if I've been waiting all my life."

"Make love to you as one vampire to another? I might well kill you, my love. You are but a babe."

"Then kill me! This is how I would die!" Grace's voice was deep and sensual with arousal, but the urgency was plain. She wanted what he offered, whatever the cost. He had expected desire, but he had not expected this. Again, their eyes locked, and he read into her soul. Yes, she wanted his love, and his blood. She wanted to suffer and be exalted in equal measure. She did not want to control, but nor would she be denied.

Julian's passion flared again, obscuring all better judgment. Slowly he raised himself over the naked willing girl, touching the head of his cock to her wet entrance. She arched herself up, seeking him out with her sex, and Julian complied, pressing into her. Grace screamed, but it was the scream of primal appetite, not of pain.

That would come next.

Chapter Ten

"Grace," he whispered over and over, but he could not rouse her. What had he done? He had listened to the entreaties of a newfound vampire, letting his own lust cloud his senses. And now she lay still as death, white as a funeral drum. "Grace," his voice broke as he leaned close to her, dropping his head gently on her bare breasts.

Dimly he could still hear her heart beating and thrumming against his ear. She yet lived! But it was by no means certain that she would regain consciousness. Even now, with his lover's life poised between heaven and earth, Julian couldn't stop the images of what they had just done together from filing past his mind's eye like a rich banquet for the senses.

He felt the warm fullness in his veins from her blood, rich and plentiful as she had just fed herself. Yes, as he had entered her with his cock, so too had his teeth bitten down. First on her breast, just above a jutting nipple, over a pale blue vein, outlined below the soft white skin. Grace had cried out as he bit her, but she didn't struggle. No, in fact, she had arched up to meet both his cock and his mouth, accepting the pleasure and the pain as one. Her submission made him perhaps bolder than he would have been, and he suckled freely, the bright-red blood dribbling down his chin when he at last let go to kiss her mouth.

The pulsing, throbbing perfection of his cock buried deep in her velvet cunt was offset suddenly as he felt the prick of a vampire lover's special kiss. Grace's sharp kiss easily broke the skin protecting the subclavian artery. Julian's first instinct was to pull away, but he forced himself to endure it. To accept the primal lover's bite that he hadn't felt for so many years — too many to count.

As she sucked his blood, her strong legs wrapped around his hips, pulling him into her. Julian felt himself grow dizzy and faint. She should stop soon. She must stop. His head grew heavy and he forgot where he was for a moment. The dizziness shifted to heightened sensation as she took more of his life's blood from him, while still moving in a tight, perfect dance on his cock.

Finally, Julian found the strength to pull away. Gently, but forcibly, he pried open the greedy girl's mouth, causing her to release her canine grip. He smelled his own blood, pungent and ripe on her tongue. She moved forward, her eyes closed as if in a trance and her fangs bared, seeking again the blood she'd waited her whole life to taste.

Julian's need overrode his charity, and he bent over her, baring her white slender neck to his own sharp kiss. He bit down, expertly drawing the blood in a steady hot stream, swallowing as rapidly as he could so as not miss a drop. Grace moaned, still impaled on his cock, held in his razor grip by the throat. Her moans became barely audible. Julian knew he should stop or at least slow down, but his lust was at a fever-pitch.

Though he'd lain with hundreds of women over the past centuries, no one had ignited his passion as this girl did, except perhaps his first real lover, Adrienne. When her writhing slowly ceased beneath him, Julian came to himself, suddenly gripped with an icy fear that he'd gone too far.

"Grace," he had whispered, "Grace, speak to me. Where are you?"

"I'm here, you silly angel, my darling," she had whispered, to his great relief. And then, to his astonishment, "Take me. I want more." She smiled slowly, her vampire fangs now fully distended and still red with his blood.

Julian, in a most uncharacteristic act, bared his own throat for his lady. She didn't need a second invitation. Biting down, she groaned against the onslaught of hot salty blood. As she suckled, her body came alive again, and she arched and thrust her hips against the man whose cock was still buried deep inside of her.

Julian was close to climax, though weakening again now from her relentless grip on his throat. She was beyond greedy. She was a blood-slut and would have to be taught. But now no words or coaching would penetrate her near-trancelike state. Instead, he again forced her lips apart, stopping the flow of his blood before he was powerless to resist her.

He pulled out of her tight little cunt at the same time, and Grace actually whimpered with dismay. No shy flower any longer. She was a wanton whore—her legs lewdly spread revealing the sticky sweet crush of her sex. Her head was thrown back on the pillows, her hair wildly cascading in shades of red and gold around her like a halo. Her lips, dark red against white skin, were parted and a thread of Julian's blood trickled from the corner. Julian's lust seized him like a sickness, and he no longer gave thought to her safety or her desires. His head pounded with bloodlust and pure animal desire.

Hoisting her roughly up, Julian forced the girl to her hands and knees. Positioning himself quickly behind her, he thrust his aching cock into her sweet, wet pussy in one long smooth movement, like a well-oiled sword finding its sheath. Grace moaned and fell forward, but Julian's strong arms were there to catch and hold her.

As he roughly fucked her from behind, his teeth sought the sweetmeat of her vein where her neck and shoulder met and he bit, like a dog rutting with a bitch in heat. Grace screamed, and Julian knew it was from both pleasure and pain. This spurred him on, and he fucked her mercilessly, ramming against her as he held her hips with his hands to keep her steady.

The blood spurting in his mouth and the tight muscles of her cunt wrapped around his cock brought him to the edge of release. The delicate curve of her long, narrow back and the globes of her rounded bottom sent him over that edge, and he cried out his passion with a single word — her name.

Collapsing against her, Julian lost consciousness for a moment or two. When he opened his eyes, his lover lay unnaturally still beneath him. Quickly he moved off her, all concern now that his greedy lust had been satiated.

Over and over, he had called her name, seeking her soul with his probing thoughts but finding nothing. When at last he'd given up, and laid his head softly against those sweet breasts, he had heard that weak but still pumping heart.

Something wet fell across her bosom as Julian lay still, and he realized with surprise that it was his own tears. Sitting up next to her, Julian stoked Grace's soft skin, whispering her name like a prayer. Her eyelids fluttered and slowly opened. Her pupils were huge, almost obscuring the pale blue-green irises. *Julian.* He heard the word in his head though she made no sound. Her lips curved into the hint of a smile, and Julian felt relief wash over him, leaving him literally weak.

Smiling down on her, Julian lay a hand on her warm thigh as if she were a square of sunlight and he just in from the cold.

* * * * *

They were lying naked together in tangled sheets, sipping champagne and speaking in the lazy soft tones of people with all the time in the world. It was a Monday, but Grace hadn't reported for work at the downtown law firm. She'd called in sick, but in fact she knew she would never return.

"You've survived the sacred exchange," Julian told her, "though my own lust almost cost you your life. I can never forgive myself for that, Grace. I realized, as you lay senseless and weakened that I couldn't bear losing you. I know, I know —" he held out his hand, palm up, as if to stop her protest, though it was in fact himself he was admonishing. "We've only just met. And yet how many have shared the intense intimacies you and I have experienced together in so short a time? It is as if we were born for one another."

He didn't ask if she felt the same way. He didn't have to. Their psychic connection was firmer than ever, now that they had shared each other's blood. Julian, who rarely slept more than a few hours at a time, had fallen into a deep sleep once Grace had been roused and he had satisfied himself that she was out of danger.

Together they slept the sleep of lovers, their bodies entwined, their dreams spilling over into their new and impossibly sweet reality. Grace awoke several times to stare at the luminous skin of her newfound lover. At his dark curls tumbling softly against his neck. At the two tiny holes, she had left as her mark on his flesh, now all but indiscernible.

Grace touched her canine teeth, which had retracted to their normal length. She had never read of this ability or reaction in the literature, but it made sense. How else could these vampires have moved so easily disguised in society? Their teeth must retain a quality not unlike other organs that distend when engorged with blood. The penis or the nipples, for example. Grace shivered a little, touching her own bare breasts and the little mark just above her right nipple where Julian had suckled so greedily.

She realized she couldn't possibly have truly absorbed the fact of her new life. Or the admission of it. To think, she had always possessed these abilities, these powers and desires and yet, had remained unaware. The years of torment and self-imposed suffering had been shed in one amazing weekend. She had sloughed it all off like an old and unwelcome skin.

What would her parents say? Julian had told her some of what to expect, now that she had finally awakened her vampire passions. She would cease to age. Well not cease precisely, but the process would be so dramatically slowed that she would not notice it from decade to decade, century to century. How to grasp such a concept! Julian looked barely thirty and yet assured her he was born just before the turn of the eighteenth century.

Was it all an elaborate and bizarre hoax? But no, how could he have feigned the psychic connection they shared? Or the sacred exchange, as he called it, of their blood? Or the life-giving exhilaration she had felt when she took her first human victim.

It had been as if she were a hollow vessel, empty and dry as a bone. When her lips and teeth made contact with that poor dying addict it was as he had said, as if a parched desert were suddenly in the most beautiful bloom. As the sweet blood pumped through her, she felt her life was renewed. The constant sickness and hunger she had carried silently for so many years in the pit of her being was snuffed out with that sharp kiss.

She had no reason to disbelieve Julian about the longevity of vampires. There was much in the literature to substantiate these claims. She was fascinated with the little snippets he had provided and eager to learn all about his rich and adventurous life.

But there was all the time in the world. What a novel thought! She laid back, content just to stare out at the constantly shifting patterns of the dark-green leaves at her windowpane. Being a practical person, one of her first questions was how did he live? He didn't seem to hold a job, and yet he was obviously wealthy and unconcerned about money.

He told her about the Dark Circle. About the Elders, and his sizable holdings in real estate and investments all over the world. "When you have a lifetime, indeed, many lifetimes, to invest and expand, you learn a great deal. I leave the handling of the day-to-day matters to trusted humans. I have been burned occasionally along the way, but one learns quickly whom one can trust."

Switching topics, as money really didn't interest him, Julian said, "You will need to meet with the Elders, you know. You're a missing piece. You've somehow slipped through the careful net of vampire society. But now that you're with me, you will be noticed. We will need to take a trip abroad, my dear. Have you ever traveled?"

"Well, I've been to New York and to Mexico for visits, but other than that, no. I've always wanted to travel but never had the means or the time."

Julian smiled. Ah, to be so new! He had traveled the world so many times that it had lost its appeal, its mystery, for him. He well understood the term travel-weary. Perhaps with Grace, he would rediscover the joys of new cultures and experiences. Seeing it all again for the first time through her eyes. "Well, you have the time now, my dear. And the means. Once you are initiated into the Dark Circle, I am sure you will be provided with your own portfolio. There are definite advantages to our situation over the poor humans. Not having to worry about financial issues is certainly one of them, but money and things rather bore me. I much prefer the company of a beautiful woman." Tenderly he touched her cheek.

Grace smiled shyly, feeling thoroughly happy. When they made love this time, no blood was exchanged. Yet, his power was evident. Grace, who had never considered herself sexually submissive, found herself drawn to his dominant ways. When he ordered her to sit back on her haunches, her fingers laced behind her head, it didn't occur to her to disobey. Indeed, it excited her to comply as he commanded that she stay perfectly still, no matter what he did to her.

"Don't move, wench. I am going to touch you as it pleases me. You are not to move or to fall out of position. Understand? Do so, and I will punish you." Grace shivered a little. She saw the twinkle in his dark eyes, but still the game felt real. Punishment! Like something out of a Gothic romance novel.

Obediently she knelt up, her pretty little breasts offered to him as the position of her arms behind her head raised them for his pleasure. Her sex was exposed beneath the auburn pubic curls as she spread her slender thighs at his direction. Julian, wearing only his jeans, his supple bare chest exposed, stood up next to the bed where his naked lover awaited his caress.

At first, he kissed and licked her little nipples, smiling as the tips sprang to attention. Gently cupping each breast in his hands, he lifted and then let them drop. When she tried to lean down to kiss him, Julian lightly slapped her cheek, startling Grace back into position. She touched the little stinging spot where he'd hit her, her eyes wide.

"I told you," he said, lightly biting a nipple between words, "to stay still. I did not say to bend down and kiss me. You will learn, my love. Though the days when a man essentially owned a woman as his personal property are gone, at least in this country, you will find that my preferences still run thus. I like to own my woman. To cherish and adore her, of course. But she is to obey me. In everything—but most especially in sex. Am I understood, wench?"

Grace's learned reaction was to balk. The words leaped to her lips that she was nobody's wench, nobody's property. How dare he speak to her, a modern American woman, with such insolence? But the words died before forming. Her body responded to his command. She knew that he was aware of her sudden rush of desire. There were no secrets between vampires on the same psychic connection.

"Yes," he murmured, his voice low. "Yes, I knew it. I sensed it in you the first time we met. You are submissive. You are untrained, but you are eager. There are so many wonderful things awaiting us, my love. I have waited so many years to find you!" He bit her nipple much harder, twisting it with his teeth. Grace gasped as the pain registered, mixing in a strange way with the tingling need pulsating now at her sex.

She was breathing hard as his hands slid sensuously down her sides, wrapping around to cup her small, round ass. She leaned forward, trying to touch his body with hers. Again, the sudden slap to her cheek, this time harder. Grace's hand flew again to her face. "Julian!" she cried.

"I gave you one simple command, dear girl. Surely, you can remember it? But if not, we shall move from a little slap to a spanking on that sweet little ass. Would you prefer that? It can be most humiliating for a grown woman to submit to such a thing. But I have done it before and will certainly do it again." He smiled, his eyes bright with lust.

"Julian, this game, I..."

"It's no game, my love. There are rules, yes, but it is no game. I told you when we met to accept your fate. Your fate as a vampire and your fate with me. We were born for one another, do you deny that?"

"No," she whispered.

"Then you must trust me. You belong to me, as I belong to you. I will lead you. You will follow and you will obey." Then he kissed her, passionately, bending her back so that she fell out of her kneeling position. His lips and tongue explored her mouth and then trailed down her throat, again teasing and suckling her nipples before moving down to her firm flat belly and the sweet bud of her sex, soft and hot to his kiss.

When he entered her, she was ready to receive him, her folds engorged with blood and wet with need. He fucked her slowly, easing in and out until she screamed and wrapped her legs around his hips, forcing him to penetrate her more fully.

"Fuck me! Fuck me!" she yelled like a wanton whore, and he eagerly complied, claiming her with his cock as he held her pinned beneath him.

Later, as they lay sticky and sweating in the late afternoon Grace murmured, "I want it." They were lying back to back, barely touching on top of the sheets. The ceiling fan whirred and clattered overhead.

"You want what?" Julian asked, though he knew.

"What you said."

"You say it, Grace. You tell me."

"I want to obey. I want to be yours."

"Ah, that is good, my love. Because you already are."

Chapter Eleven

Grace was surprised how little she had collected in her short life. They went through her things, deciding what to keep and what to store. It only came down to a few boxes of prized books and a few trinkets from her childhood. The rest of it — the used furniture, the kitchen items and most of the clothing and costume jewelry — she found she had no desire to keep.

How different the world seemed when time no longer mattered. How easy it had been to give notice at work. Because it was a large law firm and paralegals sometimes took their client information with them to rival firms, Grace was not asked to stay until they could find a replacement, but was instructed to pack her things and vacate the premises immediately.

Standing at the desk where she had spent five days a week for the past three years, she only took a moment to decide what to keep and what to toss. She pushed most of her things straight into the garbage, of course having no intention of going anywhere even remotely like another law firm as long as she could help it. She happily gave away things that used to matter to her. To her desk mate, Julie, she gave the coveted heavy-duty hole-punch, her sizable supply of post-it notes and her lucky Shamrock plant. The little magnetic sculptures she used to play with while on endless phone calls with law offices, real estate firms and corporate secretaries, she gave to Ron the mail clerk who had always admired them.

The rest of the support staff seemed to be in awe of Grace, who could just walk out with no future plans as far as they could see. If they knew the real reason she was leaving, none of them would have believed it. It saddened Grace a little to realize she wouldn't really miss any of these people. No one, she admitted now to herself, had ever made much of an impact in her life. Her mother used to say she was cold. "And after all we've done for you," she would say, shaking her head sadly. The accusation hurt, but Grace hadn't been able to project a warmth she couldn't seem to feel. She did love her parents but it never seemed to be enough. Grace knew now that it was because she was different. She just hadn't realized quite how different.

They rented a little storage room in the area, and Julian noted the information carefully in an old leather-bound notebook he carried in his luggage. "I really should get with the modern age," he said smiling. "If I lost this thing I'd lose access to a number of bank accounts, houses and storage facilities across the United States and Europe. But I've used this book for so many years it's like an old friend."

"I'm going to get you a palm pilot," Grace rejoined. "You can still carry that notebook, but we'll just enter the information in the pilot as well. Kind of a backup system."

"Fine with me, as long as you're the one to enter the information!" They laughed, and Grace was quietly pleased that she had a skill or knowledge that this learned and cultured fellow did not possess. She was also pleased that though he had told her she was to submit to him, this didn't mean he was going to treat her as something "less than". Quite the contrary. As he explained it, a submissive woman was the most exalted creature on the planet. She would be revered and debased with equal fervor.

"It's a paradox, much like the taking of blood. The intrinsic beauty of pleasure and pain, combining in an alloy much stronger than either sensation on its own. The loss of blood weakens but the giving of it strengthens the spirit immeasurably. Submission is like that, when love is a factor. And I do love you, Grace. I do."

When she took her second victim, Julian provided the distraction, but it was Grace herself who subdued the prey. This time it was a woman. A prostitute standing under a sputtering streetlamp in the gray hour just before dawn. She shouldn't have been alone, and it was only chance that she was, as the two other whores who worked that block had just gotten quickies. They were hidden in the alley, sucking the condom-covered cocks of lonely, desperate men.

Julian approached her as if to ask for her favors. The young woman perked up, flashing most of one breast as she said, "Hey good-looking. I've got just what you need."

"You do indeed," he said, his teeth flashing white in the pale light of the streetlamp.

Grace meanwhile had slipped up behind her. Silently she wrapped an arm around the woman's throat in the way Julian had taught her. Within moments, with barely a cry, the woman had succumbed, sinking back against Grace. Julian lifted the woman and they quickly moved to the chosen alley where Julian propped the woman against the wall of a crumbling building.

Grace eagerly pulled the woman over onto her lap. To think, a few weeks ago she would never even have encountered such a person — much less lay them over her lap, lovingly pushing back the brittle, over-dyed platinum hair from her neck.

Bending swiftly, her blood-thirst rising like a flame, Grace bit. She sucked deeply, choking for a moment until the pressure evened, allowing for a steady hot flow of life. Julian watched her as he stood guard, glancing each way down the dark alley with his keen eyes.

After several moments, he heard a scuffle and the sound of voices. One of the prostitutes and her john were coming around the corner. "Grace," he hissed. "Grace, stop. Let's go. They're coming."

Grace heard him and knew she must obey. They had talked much of the dangers of feeding in heavily populated areas such as this, and his dire warnings had impressed her. Oh, just another mouthful, just a little more! She felt him wrench her arm, forcing her to release her passionate grip on the woman's throat.

With great reluctance, Grace let go and allowed herself to be pulled fully upright. As she and Julian slipped away, she turned back to see the couple bending over the still unconscious woman. Would they see the tiny wound at her throat? Probably not. What would they think had happened? But their story was not for Grace to know, as Julian hurried her to his waiting rental car, a black sports car, as sleek as a panther.

Julian fed next. He left her waiting in the car with the soft strains of a jazz quartet soothing her as she sat. The sense of well-being at having fed fully was offset by a pulsing heat in her sex. A part of her had wanted to watch him on his own hunt but she didn't want to slow him down. There would time, so much time, for that later when she grew stronger and more sure of herself as she more fully claimed her birthright. Meanwhile, her desire awakened, as it always seemed to be by the hunt, she contented herself with slipping her fingers into her panties to steal a moment's pleasure.

They made love again and again, unable to get enough of one another. They kissed until their lips were raw and touched each other with tenderness and rough passion. It was several days before they dared to share the sacred blood again.

Julian noted with approval that Grace's countenance had changed since she'd begun to feed. Her skin, while still pale, had begun at last to take on the luminous shining quality of a true vampire. It was a subtle thing, but one which made her immeasurably more beautiful. She was no longer a skinny waif of a thing. The blood she had needed for so long had begun to restore her, adding a much-needed layer of fat beneath skin now dewy with health.

People stared at the girl passing by, at her long auburn and golden hair tossing as she laughed, walking beside the tall, handsome young man with the dark hair and broad shoulders. "They're in love," they would sigh wistfully.

Tonight Julian agreed to her entreaties. "I'm strong enough! I promise you, Julian. I can withstand anything you choose to give me. Please, let us share the blood again. I want your sweet, sharp kiss. I must have you!"

Julian laughed, but her words ignited his passion. He had been holding himself back in concern for her and her weakness. She did seem much stronger now. If she could withstand it when she had only fed the one time, how much easier would it now be? As Grace began a slow, sensual striptease in front of her man, Julian relented, taking off his own black T-shirt and jeans.

Grace stood in only her thong panties, black against fair creamy skin. He admired for the hundredth time her long, lean lines, broken only by the gentle flare of her hips and the round sweetness of her breasts.

Julian kissed her roughly as he bent her back in his strong arms. Her arms were bound at her sides by his embrace and she moaned, whispering, "I love that feeling of helplessness. When I can't move, when I can't resist you. My big, strong, sexy man."

Julian laughed, still holding her captive. "You're giving me an idea, my lady. How would you like to be truly helpless? Truly bound and at my mercy?" As he spoke, Julian released her, but only for a moment. Rummaging in a large trunk while Grace stood watching, he produced several lengths of thin silken rope, dyed a bright red.

"These were a gift from a Japanese lover who adored the art of nawa shibari, the Japanese term for sensual bondage. I believe I shall tie you with these bonds and render you completely helpless."

"Oh, Julian, I don't know." What had sounded sexy in theory suddenly seemed a little frightening. Especially, since they were going to share the blood. Grace began to back away, wrapping her arms around herself in that old characteristic gesture of uncertainty.

"That's all right, darling. You don't have to know. I'll do the knowing for both of us. All you have to do is obey. Now, hold out your wrists."

Grace bit her lower lip but she complied, holding out her arms to her lover, the palms and wrists touching. Julian wrapped the ropes around and between her wrists, executing a clever knot that could be easily undone but would only tighten if one struggled against it.

He used the rest of the ropes to skillfully secure his lover. She couldn't move and certainly couldn't walk, so he lifted her bound body and carried it to the huge bed in their hotel suite. He had left her pussy, ass and breasts easily accessible to his probing fingers and mouth. He proceeded to kiss and lick her exposed parts, drawing a sensual series of moans and sighs from the girl.

When she was very near to orgasm, but not yet there, he stopped, precisely aware of what he was doing. Leaning over her, he lay across her, rubbing his cock against her pussy. "Listen to me, Grace. I'm going to untie your legs and then retie them to the bedposts. You are not to struggle or move, do you understand?"

Grace nodded, trying to focus on his words. She was so close! So close and longing to slip over the edge of ecstasy. She shuddered, pushing up against his hand wantonly when it accidentally brushed her bared pussy as he repositioned her on the bed. Within a few moments, she was tethered by ropes at her ankles and thighs to the bed. Her cunt was completely exposed, spread and shining with her juices. Her arms and wrists were still securely bound.

Julian again slid over her, pressing her down with his weight. He kissed her mouth for several minutes as he ground his hard cock against her body. Then he whispered, "I'm going to take the blood, Grace. But as only a lover and a master would dare. I'm going to bite your sweet little clit, Grace. And take the blood from there."

Grace, whose eyes were shut in a state of blissful arousal tried suddenly to sit up. Her eyes flew open, and the panic was clear in her movements, in her cry and in her thoughts. "No!" she shouted, all promises of submission forgotten.

"Hush, my love, or I will be forced to gag you as well. And you'll want use of your mouth, because I plan to share my blood with you as well."

Grace stilled and lay slowly back. Her body was trembling. But the thought of his blood, slipping down her throat, flowing like fire into her veins, gave her courage. *You can trust me, my love. I adore you and would never harm you.*

I am afraid, but I do trust you. Take me as you will.

Kneeling between her legs, Julian licked and kissed at her clit, teasing it out from its hooded cloak as it engorged with blood. Grace shuddered with pleasure, but her body was rigid, poised for the sharp bite of his fangs. She couldn't suppress a little mewl of fear. When it came, she felt the piercing of tender, delicate flesh, but she was unable to move, securely bound by the thin, soft ropes.

Along with the sting of the bite, she felt the euphoria that came with the offering of the sacred blood. His long tongue continued to lick and suck at her, even as his fangs pierced her like needles. The combined sensation was almost too much to bear, and Grace began to wail, the pitch rising as she neared a searing orgasm.

Just as suddenly, he withdrew his hold and lifted himself over the bound woman, thrusting his cock against her tender center. As he entered her, his head dropped to her shoulder, his neck exposed.

Do it. He sent the message, but even without his permission, her lips were already parting, the teeth distending for her own piercing kiss. Julian groaned as she bit down, finding the sweet spot where blood gushed in a hot flow. As he thrust and swiveled inside of her, creating the perfect friction, she was transported by his offering. No longer greedily sucking, but content to let it slide down her open throat, Grace lost herself in the moment.

She no longer knew who or what she was. She was pure sensation, bound, fucked and fed liquid gold the color of life, bright and urgent. She felt herself leave her body, hovering overhead with Julian's spirit. Together they shared the blood and the passion until both fell unconscious, one bound in silk, but both bound in love.

Chapter Twelve

Grace's cell phone was ringing. Julian was out on the terrace reading a book and sipping champagne. Grace was lying on a huge couch just inside the hotel suite with her own book, feeling very peaceful. She hadn't told anyone where she was, though she had given her landlord notice and the little apartment now stood empty. To her parents, who lived over a hundred miles away, she had said she was taking a much-needed vacation with some friends, and would let them know when she returned.

They were not a close-knit family and it wouldn't have occurred to them to question her. The few friends she had knew she had quit her job and that a man was involved. It was so unlike Grace that they didn't quite know how to respond. Not that she gave them a chance to.

Every moment was spent with Julian. It was only a matter of time before they would leave the continent and begin their journey back to France, where Julian would seek out the Elders of the Dark Circle and request her initiation into the coven. Grace hadn't yet decided what to tell her parents. The truth, obviously, would never do.

Now she picked up the little phone and read the caller ID. Margo Patrick. Mistress Margo! During her intense confusion following the episode with Rhonda, Margo had been the one who had talked her through it all. She had been supportive and never judgmental. What had she said? Grace recalled now, she had told Grace there was something she needed to confront. Something about admitting her true nature. Had Margo known? Was *she* a vampire? But no, that was impossible. Julian would have sensed it. She herself would have sensed it!

She flipped open the phone and said, "Hello?"

"Hello! Grace! Where have you been? I've been calling for days!"

"Oh, I didn't realize," Grace said. In fact, she had only just picked up the cell phone from the apartment yesterday, when they'd done her final packing. She hadn't bothered to check the messages since Regan was usually the only one to leave one, and she was in Cancun at the moment with her latest conquest.

"Well, it's okay. I mainly wanted to see how you are. The way the two of you just left the dinner last week! You and the dashing Julian Gaston. You were quite the talk of the party." She paused as if waiting for Grace to respond, but Grace remained silent, clutching the little phone to her ear. Margo continued in that low, smooth voice with its particular New Orleans accent, part southern, part Brooklyn, part French. "I know about you, you know. I know what you are."

Grace felt a sudden chill. "What?" she murmured faintly.

"Grace, I know most of us are just players, including myself. We're not real vampires. We play the games and follow the made-up rules of our made-up covens because it gives us a sense of identity. For many, probably for most, it's something campy and pseudo-dangerous to do. But for others of us, for me, it's much more than that."

She paused and then said, "Can I see you? Is Julian with you? We need to talk."

Grace looked up and saw Julian standing at the sliding terrace door. "It's Margo," she whispered, covering the cell phone for a moment with her hand.

"I know," Julian said. "Tell her she can come. I was wondering when she'd call."

* * * * *

Margo sat on a large chair facing the couple. She was sipping the remarkably fine champagne Julian had graciously offered her. He and Grace looked so young and vulnerable sitting together, their eyes shining when they glanced at each other, their fingers intertwined. Yet Margo knew they were anything but vulnerable. She had sensed it in Grace and was certain with Julian.

They weren't the first vampires she had come across, but they were the first ones who would speak to her. She was certain that she had stumbled upon a vampire when she was on holiday in Ireland. She was a bit drunk, having just left a pub where she and several friends had shared one too many pints.

She was alone, on the short walk back to her little hotel when she happened to glance over at a nearby small farm. It was a moonless night but the stars were brilliant overhead. She saw two shadowy figures huddled together on the ground. At first, she thought someone was hurt and she had hurried over to offer help, though in her inebriated state she probably wouldn't have been much help at all. When she approached, she got the most peculiar feeling, the hairs on the back of her neck standing up as she peered into the starry darkness.

Standing at some distance, she watched the pair for a while, observing what looked like an old man cradled in the arms of a younger, larger man. After several moments, the younger man lifted his head and Margo unmistakably saw distended canines gleaming with red, shining in the silvery starlight. The man's face was pale, unnaturally so, she recalled.

Their eyes met for a moment, and then with a rustle and shimmer, the man seemed to melt away into the shadows. The old fellow slumped where he lay but otherwise was still. Margo had rushed over, now feeling completely sober. Gently she had prodded the man, but he remained unconscious. It was then she noticed the two little marks at his neck, from which a trace of blood shone darkly. After some moments, the man came to, confused and disoriented, but convinced he'd merely had "a slight spell".

She'd spent the rest of her two-week vacation seeking the mysterious stranger, convinced she'd seen the real thing at last. He had apparently disappeared without a trace. The old farmer remembered none of it. When she tried to tell him later what she had seen he had scoffed, muttering something about crazy Americans. When she tried to show him the little wounds at his throat, they were gone.

Margo, like Grace, had possessed a lifetime fascination with all things vampire. Though unlike Grace, Margo was thoroughly human. She owned all the vampire literary classics and knew whole sections by heart. She had also made a more serious study of the folklore and history, and unlike Grace, she had been convinced for a long time that vampires did in fact exist. Her sighting in Ireland merely confirmed long-held beliefs.

Her own obsession with blood was merely an extension of her fascination with the night stalkers. Though she pretended with the Red Covenant crowd and other role players to be a "sanguine vampire", she well knew it was just a game. It suited her sense of the dramatic and her dominant personality.

When Grace had come to their party that fateful Saturday, Margo had been struck by her pale skin and lithe grace. She had suspected something was odd about the girl, but she was made certain when Grace bent to suck Rhonda's little wound. She saw the glitter of lust in the young girl's eyes but more importantly, she saw the canines distend just as Grace's lips closed over Rhonda's thin arm.

At first, Margo thought she must have imagined it. But as she watched, fascinated, Grace's eager suckling confirmed her vague but growing suspicions as to what Grace must be. Yet, her careful probing of the girl led her to believe Grace herself didn't yet know or was denying her true nature for some reason. Margo sensed Grace's skittishness and moved with caution, not wanting to scare her away. She encouraged Grace to open up about her experience without trying to influence her.

When the group went to Jason's and Margo saw Julian Gaston for the first time, she was instantly struck by the pale, luminous beauty of his face. His sleek strength hidden beneath fine clothes attracted her but there was something else about him. Something indefinable which brought the image of Grace to her mind, and the memory of the dark stalker that night in Ireland.

She was surprised but delighted when Julian and Robert had struck up a conversation. As if following a script she would have written if she could, Robert gave the man his card and they seemed to be agreeing to meet at a later date to discuss Robert's prized little necklace.

That evening at the party, she had sensed the immediate and intense connection between Julian and Grace. Indeed, everyone noticed it, but the others just assumed it was some kind of "love at first sight". That it may have been, but Margo was reasonably certain that there was more, much more, between them.

Always blunt, she came right out with it. "I know what you are. I said as much to Grace. I know you're vampires. Before you protest, I want to say, I'm truly honored just to be in your presence."

"I appreciate your directness," Julian said, smiling a little. His eyes were dark, their expression guarded. "But aren't you afraid? If you're correct, aren't you concerned for your safety, your very life?"

"You mean you're going to suck my blood and leave me for dead? Or turn me into a slave zombie like in the old movies? No, I'm not afraid. I've researched vampires all my life. But beyond that, I have a sense about people. A sort of intuitive understanding of their natures. I am rarely wrong. And I sense in you, in both of you, a goodness. You wouldn't harm me."

"Not intentionally perhaps, but you are in fact in danger, Madam. Grave danger." Julian's tone was steely and Margo stiffened. Even Grace sat up straighter, glancing sharply at her lover. Would he harm Margo?

"If you've truly done your research, you know that vampires greatly prefer that their true identities remain a secret. We have been reviled and feared for centuries, often for good reason. I could kill you with one kiss, my dear. Surely you know that?"

"Yes," Margo whispered, her eyes wide. She was gripping the arms of her chair tightly, her knuckles showing white. He had just admitted what she already knew.

I trust you. She sent the message out wildly—testing the theories she had read in some of the literature that vampires were telepathic. *I put myself at your mercy, both of you. I want what you have. I've waited my entire life for this moment. If you are planning to kill me, do it now. If I am to die, let it be this way.*

"Margo!" Grace spoke aloud. "You don't know what you're saying." Margo smiled, and drew in a shaky breath. They had read her thoughts! She had risked everything in coming here but she couldn't have done anything else. Two vampires together! Margo had already begun to befriend Grace, and had felt confident that Grace would not harm her. Julian had been the unknown quantity and he had frightened her with his words, but still she felt in her bones that she was safe. She knew it was rare that a vampire would feed on someone known to them. The risk was too great—they would have to be prepared to kill.

Julian looked keenly at the woman sitting across from them. She had lovely features, with large brown eyes whose beauty wasn't lessened by the subtle mapping of tiny wrinkles at the corners. Her skin was olive-toned and still smooth though her jaw was less firm than when she was a girl, the skin sagging slightly. Her dark hair was streaked with silver and pulled back in a thick French twist at her neck. Her neck and throat were still supple, though Julian guessed she must be in her fifties. Her figure was generous, with ample bosom and broad hips, but she was by no means fat. Clothed in a coffee-colored silk pantsuit, she looked elegant but relaxed. Altogether, she was a very attractive woman.

"What exactly is it you want, Margo?" Julian spoke softly. "Why are you placing your life in our hands?"

"Read my thoughts, Monsieur Gaston. You will see that my heart is honest and my intentions pure. I've spent my life pursuing knowledge and hoping for glimpses of your kind. I did see another, years ago, but he vanished into the night. I sensed something in Grace, but was confused by her obvious lack of self-awareness. But I think I understand. I think she is what I've heard referred to as a 'latent' vampire. She was unaware of her own nature."

"You are learned," Julian admitted. "And yes, Grace was indeed latent, having never been trained or made aware of her own powers and needs. She is aware now, well aware." Grace nodded, smiling slightly at her lover before looking back at Margo.

"And I see in your heart and mind that you want something of us. Something we are not prepared or permitted to give."

"To be turned," Grace whispered, suddenly understanding. Her powers of telepathic perception were not yet nearly as developed as Julian's.

"Yes!" Margo interjected. "To be turned! I know the term. I've read enough stories and fables that I am convinced there is truth in this. You can take a human and give them the blood, and create a vampire! You can give me the bloodlust. You can give me the gift of eternal life!"

"No!" Julian shouted. "No, that is something we cannot do! And you don't know what you ask. To walk the world for decades, for centuries, almost always alone, hiding, attacking and sometimes killing humans to get what you need. Driven by your thirst for the red elixir, but alone, so often alone. It's not something to ask for. It's not something to seek. A vampire's life is not eternal, but it can feel so. Without love it is endless and the life of the damned."

Grace's hand slipped over Julian's, her eyes soft and filled with tears.

"God, I'm such an idiot," Margo said, "Please forgive me. My whole life I've always spoken before thinking and said just what's on my mind. It's gotten me in trouble over the years, but just as often it's gotten me what I want. And I don't ask lightly, Julian. I've dreamed of this moment for thirty years. Please don't deny me."

"Margo, even if so inclined, we cannot 'turn' you. It's not permitted. Permission has to be granted by the Elders of my circle and even then, the reason must be compelling. Turning isn't easy. It takes skill and strength, and great fortitude on the part of the human." He stopped, as if lost for a moment in a dream. Speaking in almost a whisper, he said, "I myself almost died in the process."

Margo nodded soberly, seeming for the moment to abandon her plea. Instead, she said, "Tell us, please. I'm longing to hear directly from the source. I've spent my life collecting vampire tales, what I could find of them, and trying to sort the fancy from the fact. Your stories are like lifeblood to me. If you'll permit me just to sit and listen to your story, I can think of no place I'd rather be." Her tone was respectful but eager.

Julian had already shared the tale of his turning with Grace, who said, "What harm could there be, Julian? She already knows what we are, and I sense that we can trust her. Don't you?"

Julian paused, looking keenly at Margo. Slowly he stood, advancing toward her. She looked up at him but didn't move. Julian touched her chin, forcing her to raise her face to him. Slowly his fingers slid down her neck, eliciting a little shiver from her though she didn't try to look away. A vampire's gaze can intimidate even the boldest human and Julian seemed impressed. His dark eyes bore into hers as he probed her thoughts and feelings.

At last, he sat back down. Taking a champagne bottle from its ice bucket, he refreshed their glasses before saying, "I suppose we can trust her, yes." Margo, who hadn't realized she'd been holding her breath, let it out with a gush. Julian continued, "We can share our stories with you, Margo, with the understanding that what we share stays with you. If you have the knowledge and love of vampires that you claim, then you appreciate the importance of keeping our identities and actions secret. Though you may not be afraid, I wasn't kidding when I said you should be.

"We kill people, Margo. Not that we choose to, but we feed on humans. A miscalculation or a moment of greed is all it takes to snuff out a human life. I don't think you understand the import of that. We are killers, by our very nature and you, Margo, are our prey."

Margo swallowed and nodded. If only he knew how much she desired his sharp kiss, how she longed to feel the prick of a vampire's fangs. She touched her throat but said only, "I understand, Julian. And if this is my night to die, I'm ready. Now please, let's lighten the tone a bit!" She took a long drink of her fine champagne, savoring its crisp, bubbly elegance against her tongue.

Laughing lightly she said, "It's funny, though I know you must be far older than I in actual years, I feel more like your mother than your prey. There is time to discuss those weighty topics I foolishly leaped into. For now, I would be delighted with a few tales from your rich and varied past. You could start with your turning, eh, cher?"

She smiled winningly at them both, aware that her smile was one of her best features, with her square white teeth and charming dimples in either cheek. Grace said, "I'd like to hear it again, Julian. I wasn't exactly focused when you first told me." She flushed slightly as she admitted this and Margo smiled, aware that they were lovers.

So, Julian did share his tale, describing something of his life in the French countryside in the early 1700s. He spoke of how he came to meet Adrienne, and the magic she worked on him, though at such a cost. "I was in a delirium for three days, so they tell me. When I awoke the first thought on my mind was of her and the first words from my lips were her name, over and over, Adrienne..." Julian's voice faded away as he seemed lost in a time long ago. His eyes were sad as he stared, unseeing, into the fading night sky beyond the terrace doors.

Grace, who had remained quiet, seemingly as riveted as Margo by the vampire's narrative, shifted a little now and looked away. Margo saw the emotions fleeting over her face and recognized that most useless and dangerous of emotions—jealousy.

Well, who wouldn't be jealous of such a rival lover as this rich and elegant Adrienne, immortal and devastatingly sexy, to hear Julian tell it. Margo smiled a little, thinking how typical a man he was, even if he did have three hundred years of experience. Clearly, he still clung to his romantic notion of this woman, this vampire who in a fit of lustful passion had almost killed him, had "turned" him without warning or consideration and then, after a one-night stand, had simply vanished off the face of the earth.

Watching Julian, these thoughts raced through Margo's mind and she reached over to touch Grace's hand. Julian had obviously obsessed over his story for centuries, no doubt enhancing Adrienne's beauty and passion as the lonely decades passed. Margo bit her tongue to keep from voicing her opinion that this French countess probably couldn't hold a flame to Grace. Instead she said, "Why, look at the way the sun is setting on Grace's hair. It looks positively golden, as if it were liquid fire."

"Oh," Grace said, a hand rising to touch her soft lustrous hair. The sun was indeed at just such an angle that it caught the golds and reds that streaked through Grace's hair. It had the desired effect of making Julian turn from his inward thoughts to focus on his very real and alive lover sitting now before him. He smiled at her, his eyes losing the dark brooding cast they'd held a moment before.

"I'll bet this human is hungry," he said, his voice light now. "Maybe we should go get something to eat. I'm rather partial to coconut shrimp."

"Oh, and I love fried bananas!" Margo's voice took on a rapturous tone. She could almost taste the fried bananas, swimming in melted butter and brown sugar with rum, ladled over a large scoop of French vanilla ice cream. She laughed as the two vampires stared at her and admitted, "I come by this figure honestly, my friends. I love to eat! Especially dessert." They all laughed—standing and smoothing their clothing, the somber mood broken.

Margo began to spend time with the young couple, stopping by their hotel suite after work and enjoying hours of talk and reflection. Julian did most of the talking, which suited both women. Night after night, they asked endless questions, not only about his experiences as a vampire, but about history itself.

"This is incredible," Margo said, her eyes shining. "Imagine the amazing book we could write! Volumes of books! You're a walking historical gold mine. You were there! During the decline of the Ottoman Empire! The French Revolution! The forming of the United States! The Civil War. The Industrial Revolution. World War One and Two. You've been there, the silent observer of it all. Your perspective is perhaps dark, forced as you've been by your nature and your appetites to live on the edge of things. But that could be a good thing! Your observations would be unique. I could help you! Why, that's what I do. I'm an editor. I edit romances, but that doesn't mean I don't know my history. I just know we could get you published. No question about it. We would turn the world on its ear!"

"That's enough," Julian's tone was sharp, and Margo's mouth snapped shut, the color draining suddenly from her face. He spoke quietly but underneath was steel. "It was understood, was it not, that these stories and memories were to go no further than this room? Has our trust in you been misplaced, Margo? Have you steered us into a corner, the only way out of which is to kill you?"

Margo gasped as Julian continued, "I don't like to kill, Margo. But I won't hesitate, not now that we are no longer discussing only my safety but the safety of my lover, of the woman I've been waiting ten lifetimes to find. You are threatening me, us, with your remarks, whether or not they are in jest."

"Oh, my God," Margo whispered. "I'm so sorry. You're right. I'm such a blithering idiot. Such a dope. Of course, you can't write the story. Of course, I wouldn't dream of compromising you like that. It was just a fantasy. Please forgive me. I've lived in these little fantasies all my life. Sometimes I forget what's real and what's possible. I'm so, so sorry." Her eyes were brimming with tears and inside she was screaming curses at herself.

"I think you should go now, Margo. There will be other evenings."

"Yes, thank you, Julian. And Grace. Thank you for everything. I do hope we will see one another again." With heavy heart Margo stood, remarkably graceful despite her voluptuous frame. She kissed Grace on both cheeks, European style. Without meeting Julian's eyes, she thanked them once again and disappeared.

Chapter Thirteen

Margo stayed away for four days. She didn't call or drop by though she was dying to do both. How she had cried and cursed on the drive home from their hotel. She had blown the most amazing opportunity of her life. It was quite possible they would never agree to see her again. For all she knew, they had already packed their bags and were heading for Europe. They had trusted her with secrets that perhaps no other human had been privy to.

And what had she done? Dove in like an eager puppy into a summer stream, splashing and panting like a little fool. Why, oh why couldn't she keep her mouth shut! Though with Julian, her thoughts were an open book as well. Grace was beginning to explore her own telepathic abilities but evidently, that wasn't something that came overnight.

Patience, Margo admonished herself. *Perhaps if I give them space, let them see I can wait, they will call me back into their blessed circle. Their dark, delicious circle.* A day passed, two, three and four. Nothing.

Loneliness and frustration drove her back into the arms of her coven, the Red Covenant, where Robert, Rhonda and her poor, dear Mark seemed suspended in time, still playing their little games with blood and submission. Mark knelt at her feet as she entered, almost sobbing in his gratitude at her return.

"Mistress," he sighed. "I thought you were never coming back! I need to give you my blood, Mistress. Please accept my submissive offering." Margo resisted her urge to shake his arms from her leg. It wasn't his fault she had ruined everything with the vampires.

It wasn't Mark's fault that she now found their little games amusing perhaps, but nothing more. She certainly wasn't in the mood to take his feeble offering of a few drops of blood. If she had played her cards right, it might have been *her* blood being accepted by one of the true kin, as Julian had called himself and Grace.

If only she had something to offer them. A peace offering, perhaps. But what in the world did she have that they would want? Julian was obviously extremely wealthy. The two of them could have whatever they wanted. Not that they could be bought. She sighed aloud, her thoughts looping in frustrated circles.

Robert entered the large old parlor. "Margo. How nice to see you. It's been too long." His tone was formal and it was clear he was miffed. Though he didn't know where she had been, he liked for the members of the Red Covenant to spend their time with him. Where Margo enjoyed the game, for Robert it had become a way of life. He held no job, his inheritance permitting him a life of leisure, and his nature embracing a life of ease.

Having no career or vocation, his identity was completely wrapped up in the Red Covenant, and Margo's absence over the past week had probably been perceived as a kind of defection. Or so she interpreted as she took in his haughty but wounded expression. The boy really was so young, she reminded herself, not yet even out of his twenties. While he could be a prig, he really wasn't a bad fellow and she recalled that she'd spent many an enjoyable evening here with all these strange misfits, hashing over their theories about vampires, taking the blood of the submissive donors and eating Robert's food and drinking his wines.

Smiling, Margo opened her arms as she moved toward Robert, leaving poor Mark kneeling on the carpet. "Robert, darling. Forgive me for staying away so long. I had appointments. Things I just couldn't put off. I would have phoned but I got too involved. You know me. I get into a manuscript, and the rest of the world could be on fire and I wouldn't notice!"

She embraced his tall thin form, aware of the effect her breasts would have on him as she pressed closely against his chest. Robert responded, wrapping his own arms around her and briefly nuzzling her neck. "Well, it's about time you came back to the circle, Margo. Mark here's been without a mistress, and you know he likes to donate only to you."

Margo glanced back at Mark, still kneeling on the carpet with his blond head bowed, and quashed her impatience. "Yes, yes, of course. Poor Mark. Go get yourself ready, boy. I'll take some blood in a little while. I'm famished for it." She threw back her head dramatically, trying to get into the spirit of things but the game had lost its appeal. How could this charade ever compare to the time she had spent with real vampires?

Suppressing a sigh, she stood back from Robert and said, "How have you been, Robert? How is Rhonda?" She didn't hear his response. All at once, her eyes lighted on the queer, little glass vial he wore about his neck on the fine gold chain. She remembered Julian's description of the little vial Adrienne had used to sever her own vein as an offering to her lover.

Now she gazed at the little vial, its glass opaque and rainbowed from oxidation and age. Could it be the original amphora? The very one that had cut Adrienne's flesh almost three hundred years ago? How did Robert come to have such a thing? What would Julian give to have it himself? Would it gain her reentry into the heady and wonderful, if dangerous, world of the vampires?

"Robert," she spoke low, her voice seductive. "Robert, can we talk, darling? Alone?"

Robert looked confused for a moment. Though Margo knew he carried a torch for her, she had never given him the slightest provocation to go after her. She was, after all, old enough to be his mother. While she did keep Mark on a little string, their relationship was Mistress and donor. She had certainly never had sex with him, or led him to believe he was her lover. Mark had seemed content with what she offered, which was the sucking of his blood from time-to-time, and allowing him to rest his sweet corn-yellow head on her lap for stroking.

Her status as a widow these past five years had left her in a sort of bubble, sexually speaking. She had had a few dalliances, but nothing lasting and certainly nothing with a younger man. There seemed so little point to it, as her body had seemed to shut down when Roger had contracted and then died from pancreatic cancer. The idea of casual sex had at first offended and then just bored her. Usually she found she would rather be alone in bed with a good book. No one would ever replace Roger.

Now she glanced from Mark to Robert. Robert was a more complex man, and less easy to subdue. She would have to use all her wiles to get what she wanted. As she touched his forearm, squeezing just a little, she whispered, "Your bedroom perhaps? Would that be all right?"

Margo was aware that Rhonda wasn't home, as she went to see her ailing father every evening to prepare his dinner before returning to the old mansion on Charles Street to serve her "vampire" circle. She felt a stab of guilt at what she was about to do, but also felt she was serving a higher purpose now. She would do whatever it took to get back into the good graces of the vampires, whatever the cost.

Now she led Robert into his own bedroom and sat on the edge of the bed, leaning back so that her ample cleavage was clearly in view, her luscious breasts pressed together alluringly in the low-cut, soft cotton top she was wearing. "Sit next to me, Robert. You know, ever since you and that Julian fellow were discussing this little trinket of yours—" she touched the ancient amphora lightly, smiling coyly at the young man, "—I've been thinking what a pretty little thing it is. I do so love oxidized glass, you know. I wonder where I could get something like it. Don't you think it would be pretty, right here?"

She took his hand, holding his fingers lightly at her chest, just above her breasts. She licked her lips, gazing up at him through her lashes, feeling at once foolish and playful. Could she still seduce a man at her age? A man half her age? Still holding his fingers against her chest, Margo drew them down lower, until they were touching her soft full breast.

Robert gulped, his Adam's apple visibly bobbing. "Margo, what…"

She interrupted him, putting a finger to his lips. "Hush, Robert. Don't speak. Do you think maybe you could lock the door?" When he stood and strode to the bedroom door, turning the old-fashioned lock, she knew she had him. Men were so easy, she thought. Maybe she hadn't lost her touch.

Am I a whore, using my body to get what I want? This thought flitted past her, no doubt a remnant from her Catholic upbringing. What was a little casual sex, when she had the key to a three hundred-year-old vampire's desires? Her only qualm was about Rhonda, who actually seemed to be in love with this callow lad. Well, hopefully the old adage that what Rhonda didn't know wouldn't hurt her would hold true.

Margo realized that she had decided at this moment that her days with Red Covenant were over. She could no longer play the game. It was absurd in the face of what she now knew about Julian and Grace. A whole world of dreams and fantasy had suddenly become real and she could never return to this little wannabe club of pretenders.

Focusing on the task at hand, Margo said, "Robert, I've always found you so attractive. Isn't that silly? An old woman like me."

As she had hoped, he took his cue, assuring her that she wasn't old and that he had always found her sexy. "Sexy as hell," he reiterated as he sat down again, his thigh boldly touching hers. "Though I admit I'm surprised. I've known you for over two years now, and I had no idea you were even the slightest bit interested in me."

"Well, I know you're taken."

"What, Rhonda? She belongs to *me*, not the other way around. I can do what I like. And right now, I like you, Margo. Oh, my yes." As he spoke, his voice lowered and softened, his hand stroking her breast with increasing boldness.

Margo closed her eyes. Robert wasn't a man she would have chosen, even if they were the same age, but his hand did feel nice, gently caressing her flesh. She stayed very still, her eyes closed, as his hand groped inside of her top, slipping past the satin of her bra.

When he touched a nipple, she jumped a little. No one had touched her so intimately for such a long time. She hadn't realized she'd missed it. When she jerked, Robert pulled his hand away and stood up suddenly. Margo opened her eyes and saw she had sent the wrong signal.

Smiling in what she hoped was a seductive manner she said, "I'm sorry, cher. You startled me. I not used to such a handsome young man touching me like that. Please, do it again."

Robert's pupils were dilated and a flush was creeping up his cheeks. When her eyes dropped to his crotch the final evidence of his arousal was abundantly clear. As he touched her nipples again, this time with both hands, she dared to place on hand gently on his bulging pants.

Robert moaned and said, "My God. I can't believe this. I've fantasized about it forever. I had no idea. No idea." He sounded so earnest and so needy that Margo felt another stab of guilt, this time for him. She was definitely leading him on, as she had no intention of ever going past this one time. It was just a way to get the amulet.

Well, at least she would make this one time something sweet, she decided. She stood, pressing her full body against Robert's thin one, feeling his iron-hard erection poking at her belly. Aware that she didn't have much time before Rhonda returned home, she knelt quickly, pulling down the zipper of his black pants with some difficulty past his engorged member.

Robert helped her, stumbling a little, as he danced out of his pants. His cock was sticking straight up, the head popping out of the top of his bikini briefs. His cock was long and thin, like the rest of him. Margo leaned up, pressing her breasts against his shaft, rubbing it between them until he moaned.

"Oh, God, Margo, take off your top. Please. Show me those gorgeous tits." Margo obliged, hoping the blush she felt creeping over her cheeks didn't show. She felt like a young girl and was mentally chiding herself to get a grip. What if this young man, so used to his thin and nubile girlfriend, found her repulsive, fat?

She had never considered herself fat, but she was a big woman—Rubenesque, her husband used to say. She pushed the thought of Roger out of her mind and focused on the young man before her. Obviously, the boy was aroused and hopefully too far gone to care if her breasts sagged a little or her bottom was too large.

Taking the hem of her shirt in either hand, Margo lifted it over her head and shook her long silver-streaked hair loose. She unclasped the little hooks at the back of her bra and slid it down her arms. "Oh," Robert said, his mouth remaining open as he knelt now in front of her, lifting a heavy breast and putting it to his mouth.

His appreciation was evident as he suckled and licked at her nipples, now dark red and fully distended from his attentions. It felt wonderful and Margo finally let go of her own fears and insecurities as Robert lifted her again to a standing position and took her in his arms.

He kissed her deeply, his mouth wet and eager against hers. She realized with a little shock that she didn't like his kiss. His breath smelled of garlic, and his kiss was too sloppy. Gently she disengaged, dropping down again at his feet to take his cock into her mouth. As she pulled down his underwear, he kicked it aside in his impatience for her mouth.

The penis was long and difficult to take in fully, so she licked and teased up and down the shaft, circling the head with little butterfly kisses. She cupped his balls in her hand, and wrapped the other hand around the base of the shaft so that there was less to take into her throat.

Robert moaned and arched against her. "Sweet Jesus, Mary, mother of God," he cried, prompting her to shush him.

"Robert! The others!" Robert clapped a hand to his mouth like a little kid and then grinned. His hair, normally brushed severely back from his forehead, had flopped over, making him look even younger than he was. He really was a sweet boy, when he dropped all the lordly vampire posturing and affectations. Slowly she took his cock again into her mouth.

After a few moments Robert said, "I'd rather put it somewhere else. I want you so much, Margo. Please." His voice was yearning, almost pleading. Margo was put off by it, as she liked a man who took what he wanted rather than begging for it. Nonetheless, this wasn't her lover. This was a mission.

Refocused on that idea, she said, "Robert. I was wondering. Do you think I might be able to buy this from you?" Again, she touched the amphora, dragging her red nails down his chest as she did so. "It would go so perfectly with several of my outfits. I know it was expensive. I'm ready to pay whatever it cost you and more, of course, for your troubles."

Robert's hand closed over the little glass vial. "This. Yes, you mentioned you liked it. That guy Julian Gaston liked it, too. So he said, before he bloody well disappeared with Grace. Stole her, is what he did. I was going to consider allowing her to apply for a position in our circle, you know, before she blew it by going off with that loser."

Margo saw that his penis was starting to wilt. She stood and began to slowly remove her pants, revealing her pretty, satin underwear. Robert's attention was diverted as he watched her. "Oh, well," she said casually, trying to quell her nervousness about removing her underwear. "If she doesn't come back, she wasn't worthy of your attentions, Robert. The Red Covenant isn't for everyone, you know. Only the most select few."

Robert smiled, mollified. His jaw dropped a little as she slid out of her panties and stood naked before him. She blushed again as he stared openly at her sex, at her breasts. To avoid that avid gaze, she dropped onto his bed and held out her arms. Robert stripped off his briefs and tumbled heavily against her, his cock slapping her thigh.

"So about that little trinket," she murmured, as he tried to kiss her.

"It's not a little trinket, Margo. It cost me nine hundred dollars."

"I had no idea!" Margo rejoined, though in fact she herself had surmised it to be worth far more, if it was as old as she thought it was.

"Well," he said self-importantly. "It's not as if I can't afford it, you know."

Margo resisted a snort at what she felt was his bad taste. She tried again, "Well, it would make a lovely gift for someone. Someone who would appreciate its value."

Someone like me. Too bad he couldn't receive telepathic suggestions from her, a mere human. Instead, she forced herself to kiss him, allowing him to slobber and suck at her mouth.

He pressed his hard body against her yielding one and said, "I want to fuck you. Now."

"But, Robert, what about Rhonda? I think you're just using me. I'm just handy while she's out. You care nothing for me."

"But I do! I do! And you're so gorgeous. I'm going to come on your leg if you don't let me stick it in." Charming imagery, she thought grimly, though she smiled at him.

"You do care about me?" her voice was consciously coquettish.

"I do. Here." He reached behind his neck, doing the very thing she had willed. Lifting the long gold chain over his head, he handed Margo the coveted ancient glass. She took it quickly, setting it aside so he wouldn't focus on it.

"You do care," she murmured, as she pulled him onto her, guiding his bone-hard cock into her pussy. For the several minutes he lasted, it felt good. The earth didn't move, but the sensations were pleasant and it was nice to have a man again, even if she was only using him, and he her.

"Margo!" Robert cried, as he spurted into her. "Oh, Margo. That was heaven on earth. I think I'm in love."

"Silly boy," she chided softly, smoothing back his ruffled hair.

Dropping her hand to the nightstand, she felt for the little priceless trinket. She had what she wanted.

Chapter Fourteen

Margo stood at the door to their suite for several moments before daring to knock. The concierge, familiar with her frequent visits during the prior weeks, had smiled and waved her to the elevator—aware she was the guest of the very wealthy and freely tipping Monsieur Gaston.

For the hundredth time she touched the little box in her pocket. She'd wrapped the ancient treasure in it to present to Julian as a gift. A peace offering. A way back into their lives, she fervently hoped.

She heard sounds within, some kind of scuffling. Her knuckles rapped lightly at the door. No response, though she could hear that someone was inside. On a lark, she twisted the doorknob, a large, brass, old-fashioned affair. To her surprise, it turned. Slowly she pushed it open, calling out timidly, "Hello? Julian? Grace? Are you here?"

No answer but now she heard muffled sounds coming from the large master bedroom. Feeling trepidation, but too eager to see them to resist, she entered the suite and called out again. "Hi. It's me, Margo. I have something for you."

She walked to the bedroom door and stopped in shock, taking in the scene before her. The young lovers were naked, kneeling up together on the bed, their arms locked around each other, their mouths on each other's necks. Their bodies were splendid, like perfect alabaster statues, marred only by thin lines of blood trickling where their fangs met flesh.

The world seemed to take on a dreamlike quality as Margo realized what she was witnessing. They were sharing the sacred blood. She heard Julian's voice in her head, as she recalled his stories of such sharing between vampires. The potent exchange apparently strengthened and invigorated the participants, if it didn't kill them in the process.

They looked beautiful molded together in their dark kiss, touching at the mouth, their bodies angled away from each other so that they formed a little pyramid. Still lost in the dream of the moment, Margo began shedding her clothing. Without a thought to her weight or her age, or the tolls of gravity, she pulled the sarong top over her head and slipped out of her black silk pantaloons.

Off came her matching satin panties and bra. Margo felt herself pulled toward them as if she had been hypnotized and had no thought or choice in the matter. Slowly, gracefully, she moved toward the lovers and slid beneath them on the bed, offering herself, though she knew not precisely how or why.

They drew apart, their mouths rich with bright red blood. Grace's high perfect breasts were tipped with rigid nipples and Julian's thick, large cock still touched her belly though they had pulled away from each other.

Margo closed her eyes, wondering if this were the moment of her death. To disturb such an intimate act must surely be paid for with her life. And yet, Margo felt a curious peace descend over her. If this was her time, she was ready. Perhaps Roger was waiting for her somewhere, though she'd never really believed in heaven.

She lay still, feeling a warmth emanating out from her breasts and her sex. She felt good, she felt beautiful. She felt ready to die. When strong arms lifted her up between them, she didn't struggle or even open her eyes.

When sharp little teeth bit down on the soft sweetbread of her throat, she did little more than utter a soft cry. It didn't hurt exactly. It was more like a sting but along with it came a curious arousal. Was this what it was like for her little Mark? Surely not. That was playacting.

She, Margo, was being bitten by a vampire. A vampire in the throes of lust who would probably suck her blood until he took every drop. She felt something on her face, on her lips. *Open your eyes.* She heard the words resonate in her head. Slowly she obeyed only to see Julian in front of her. He leaned toward her, kissing her lips with his, soft and warm.

Eagerly she parted her lips, welcoming his velvet tongue as he kissed her. Then he wasn't biting her throat! And yet, even still she felt the sweet sting. Grace! Twisting her head back, Margo saw the young woman's pretty auburn hair spreading now over her bare shoulder and breast as she suckled at her neck.

Again, Julian's mouth was on hers as his hands found and kneaded her large breasts. She was sandwiched between the two vampires, held up by their strong, beautiful naked bodies. Letting her head fall, she closed her eyes as dizziness overtook her. Yes, she was going to die, but what a perfect way for her to go. As inky blackness softly lowered its curtain, she smiled and whispered, "Roger."

* * * * *

"Oh look, she's waking up." Grace hovered over Margo, who still lay sleeping peacefully between the fine linen sheets. Margo opened one eye and saw the two of them standing over her, both fully clothed.

Julian grinned at her and said, "Sorry, looks like you'll be sticking around for a while longer, Margo."

"What?" she murmured groggily.

"Your little fantasies about your romantic death did not come to pass, I'm afraid."

Margo turned her head on the pillow, obviously embarrassed. Even in his lustful and trance-like state, Julian had felt Margo's melodramatic musings drifting in her mind, though he hadn't processed the words until later.

What a risk she had taken! Her fears of death were in fact well founded. To interrupt vampire lovers in their passion was a dangerous move indeed. Only because she had arrived at the tail end of their sacred revelry did she survive. Hours of impassioned lovemaking and sharing of the blood had left the lovers elated but exhausted. Together over the weeks, they had learned to walk the delicate balance of sharing blood without taking so much that life became too fragile.

They made love during the days and prowled the seedy, darker parts of the Big Easy by night. Grace continued to hone her skills as a hunter. Julian had watched with pride and growing love as Grace grew stronger, learning the subtle art of taking human blood without killing her prey.

When Margo had intruded, they were so deeply involved in the sensual sacred ritual that she would have had to set off a bomb to deter them. Instead of striking out at her, as might have happened earlier in the sharing, they took her into it as a part of the whole.

Grace took her blood, yes, biting because it was offered, not because she was hungry for it. Indeed, they had been gorging themselves a little too freely in this southern town. It was beginning to make the news that so many homeless people and addicts were being found unconscious and weakened and occasionally dead, their very blood seeming to have seeped away without a trace.

Up until now, Julian had always been very careful when seeking his human victims. New love and the desire to strengthen Grace after her years of self-imposed starvation had made him reckless. They would have to be very careful going forward. Julian sensed that the time was nearing to depart this city and this continent. He felt the travel lust coming upon him and this time he had a mission.

Margo opened both eyes and smiled weakly at the two vampires stilling leaning over her. "Am I alive?" she whispered.

"Oh, Margo, of course you are." Grace sat next to the older woman. Grace's smile faded as she added, "Lucky for you I wasn't too thirsty."

"Have you ever heard of knocking?" Julian added, sitting on the other side of her. Margo struggled to sit up. As the sheets slipped down, revealing her bare breasts she blushed and grabbed at the covers, pulling them up to her chin.

Julian glanced into her mind and realized she had no memory of what happened after Grace's teeth found their mark. She didn't remember the three of them falling together, Grace's lips locked in their vampire kiss as

Margo fell back against her naked body. Margo laid half-atop Grace as Julian leaned over both of them. How natural it had felt to press his penis into Margo's wet, hot pussy.

As he slid it into her, he leaned over her to find Grace's face. As he pummeled and fucked the human, he kissed his lover's eyes, her cheekbones, the top of her head. Margo was nothing more than an object at that moment. Some lovely hot flesh to be used as they pleased. An extension of their lovemaking.

Though a powerful vampire, his stamina was flagging from the hours of heated sex with his lover. It felt good to move inside the woman beneath him, feeling the velvet clutch of her vaginal muscles, but he was too spent to orgasm.

Instead, he watched Grace sucking at her neck, her own body half-covered by Margo's larger one. They were both beautiful women, though so different. Grace, with her fair coloring and reddish-gold hair, with her high, pale breasts and long, slender body. Contrasted against her was Margo, curvy and voluptuous, with heavy breasts capped by large dark nipples, her skin a smooth olive-tan.

As Grace sucked, Julian peered at Margo's face, which was beginning to pale. Her eyelids fluttered partially open, revealing only the whites as they rolled back in her skull. He felt her thoughts still and her heart slow. Grace showed no signs of stopping her lethal kiss. Slipping his cock from its sweet embrace, Julian inserted two fingers at the corners of Grace's mouth, gently forcing her to release her death grip.

When Grace let go, Julian saw her fangs, red with blood, slowly retract as her head lolled back in a swoon. He felt himself overcome with fatigue. With his last remaining strength, he pulled Margo off the younger woman and rolled her gently to one side of the large, king bed. Slipping between the two women, he fell into a deep sleep.

"I feel very odd," Margo was saying, drawing Julian back to the moment. "I can't quite say how I came to be in your bed naked and asleep! I can only say I hope it was fun!" she grinned sheepishly.

"You don't remember, do you?" Grace said. As Margo shook her head, Grace added, "Maybe it's just as well. Some things aren't meant for humans to be involved in, or witness to."

"Oh, listen to you," Margo laughed. "You've only known you were a vampire for a month and now you're going all high and mighty on me. You sound like Robert Dalton, for heavens' sake." Then she remembered. The amphora.

"Oh, my God. My clothes. Where are my clothes?"

"Still in the heap where you dropped them, you slut," Julian laughed.

Margo clutched at the sheet again, looking thoroughly mortified. Julian took pity and said, "Oh, don't looked so worried, Margo. You probably did the best thing you could have done. I don't know if I would have let you return any other way. You really shook me with your sudden threats to reveal our secrets to the world. I could have killed you. I considered it seriously.

"But coming to us as you did, naked and vulnerable, offering yourself so sweetly between us. Well, all I can say is all is forgiven. Provided—" his voice took on a sterner tone, "—that you never breathe a word about our true natures or what we do to any other human. Is that understood, woman?"

"Yes, sir," Margo said meekly. "I've spent the last miserable week repenting. You have no idea the agony I suffered at the thought that I would never see either of you again. I couldn't work—I couldn't sleep—I couldn't even eat. Me, not eat! Unheard of!" She laughed a little but continued, "I didn't think you would ever permit me in your presence again. Or if I did dare to show up, I knew you might kill me outright, to protect your secrets. Not that I blame you! But, Julian, oh, Julian, I have something that I hope will make it right between us. Or at least better. A peace offering, that's how I think of it. A gift from me to you."

Julian smiled at her. "What could you possibly have of value that I could want? Forgive me if I seem boastful, but I can buy whatever I want whenever I want."

"You can if it isn't already owned by someone else, you mean."

"What are you saying?"

"Let me show you. Where are my clothes?" Grace went to fetch her things. Margo took them gratefully from her, feeling inside the pants pocket for the little box. She looked at the two of them and said, "Uh, excuse me, do you think I could have a little privacy to get dressed?"

Now Julian roared, throwing back his head in laughter. Grace laughed, too. "Really, Margo. You threw yourself naked at us while we were making love, and now you're feeling modest?"

"Oh, my, what did I do? I really can't recall." Margo looked thoroughly confused. Julian had observed that it was a unique and rather useful property of the act of taking the blood that the donor was usually struck with a loss of memory of the events just prior to and during the actual act. This explained why so many victims had no recollection of what happened to them and would deny it even in the face of witnesses.

Bluntly he said, "You entered our hotel suite uninvited and unannounced. You stripped off your clothes and climbed in between us. You let Grace suck your blood while I fucked you as you lay atop my lover." Margo was scarlet now.

"I don't know what to say," she whispered.

"You don't have to say anything, dear," Grace soothed, touching Margo's hot cheek. "Julian and I are so certain in our love that we have room for others. It was fun to have you with us. Next time I want to try it without sucking your blood, as that is quite a distraction."

"A distraction! You almost killed her, Grace," Julian admonished, but he was laughing. The hilarity of the odd situation suddenly seemed to strike them all and they laughed with raucous joy until tears rolled down their cheeks and they could laugh no more.

In the comfortable silence that followed, Margo eventually said, "I guess it's silly to be so modest when we're already so, uh, well acquainted." She stood up, revealing her lush naked form. Gracefully, she slipped on her underclothing while Julian and Grace watched her. Donning her loose-fitting silk pants and tying the top in place across her breasts, she sat back down on the bed and said, "There. That's better. I don't like to be the only one naked."

She touched the pocket of her pants and slipped her fingers into it, withdrawing a little box the color of a robin's egg. "For you, sir," she said in a low voice.

Julian accepted the gift with a slight inclination of his head, holding it a moment before he opened it. Slowly he slipped off the dark blue ribbon that adorned the box and lifted the lid. He stared at its content for a long moment, his expression inscrutable.

Lifting it carefully from its cotton nest, Julian held the little vial cradled in his palms. "Thank you," he said simply, though the gratitude was clear behind the two little words. He turned to Grace, who watched him with large eyes, her thoughts concealed from Margo but not from her lover.

"My little fool," he whispered, smiling gently. "She is but a memory. You needn't fear a dream, my love. You are my present and my reality. This thing—" he held the little amphora by its golden chain so that it sparkled in the light for a moment, "—is just a symbol. A beautiful piece of ancient glass." He stood and walked around the other side of the bed to Grace, who looked up at him and nodded slowly, obeying his silent command.

Lifting her heavy mane of hair from her long, slender neck she bent forward slightly so that he could attach the chain around her neck. "A gift from Robert to Margo to me to you. And it suits you, Grace. Its fragile beauty belies its strength, its power to cut and take the blood. Just like you." Grace smiled, and touched the little vial, her eyes still on Julian.

Turning to Margo, he said, "I won't even ask how you got this, Margo."

As blood suffused her cheeks again, she shook her head in exasperation and said, "My God, I haven't blushed this much since high school! All I will say is, I never kiss and tell."

"Well, that's good to know," Grace said. They all stared at each other for a moment before the second wave of hilarity broke over them, leaving them weak with it.

Chapter Fifteen

The tickets were purchased and time was running out. Julian had made it clear that he and Grace were leaving by the end of the week. As he explained to Margo, he felt the danger creeping up. New Orleans was no longer a safe haven for the likes of them. He had learned years ago never to disregard his intuition in these matters. When Margo had asked if she could go with them, at first he had been surprised. Humans didn't usually drop everything and take off the way vampires did. They didn't have that luxury, as a rule.

Margo had pleaded, saying that she sensed this was the time in her life she had been waiting for. It was almost as if she had been suspended, waiting to begin to live again, since Roger had died. Connecting with Grace and Julian, she said, had somehow turned her back on to life. She didn't want to let the opportunity pass her by.

Gently Julian had refused her. "I'm so glad you feel able to begin living again, Margo. We feel honored to have been a part of the renewal of your spirit. But you are not of our kind. We are going where you cannot follow. We will seek the Elders. We are beginning a new journey together." He turned toward Grace, his eyes shining with love.

Despite her ardent desire to share the adventure, Margo understood that these new lovers needed time to themselves. She knew she was shockingly selfish to try and insinuate herself into their little circle of two. And yet, the longing persisted. And the secret and continuing desire to be "turned", to become one of them.

As the last days slipped by, Margo found herself always in their penthouse suite. Though they did not make love again with her, she found it exciting and at the same time, comforting just to be near them. On some level she felt more kindred to these vampires than to her own kind. Yet, Julian remained steadfast that she could not accompany them on their trip to Europe.

"We will come back, or call for you when the time is right, Margo. We have something special between us three. We won't forget you." Grace promised, giving Margo something, however slender, to cling to.

* * * * *

"Where have you been these past weeks, Margo? We barely see you!" Robert's voice was peevish, his expression petulant.

Forcing her face to relax into a smile Margo answered, "I've been very busy, Robert. Got a big edit to finish and the author is such a pain in my ass! Published one book before this one, to moderate success and now thinks she's a writing diva!"

Robert muttered something, clearly not satisfied with her explanation. Mark appeared from the kitchen, his face bursting into a happy smile at the sight of his mistress. Turning toward him, Margo's smile became genuine. She really did love Mark, in her own way. He was so simple and his devotion to her so unflagging.

As he knelt, she smoothed his hair and bent down to kiss his forehead. "Mark, cher. Are you our swan tonight?" Mark was dressed in a tight T-shirt that showed off his heavily muscled chest and arms. He was a good-looking man. Her newfound lust that had been awakened in the arms of Julian and Grace came to the fore, and she felt something like arousal for this younger, sexy man.

"Yes, mistress," he sighed happily.

"That's right," Robert interjected. "We're having a double bloodletting. Rhonda and Mark. And we're having several new guests. People *want* to join this circle, you know, Margo. People who won't take its membership for granted."

She let it pass. She'd only come tonight out of guilt, and because Julian and Grace were off hunting and never permitted her to join them. This was their last night in New Orleans. Just the thought of not knowing when or if she would see them again made Margo almost physically ill. She had even briefly considered secretly following them, but believed Julian that his wrath would know no bounds if he found she had done so. "We will come for you, Margo, when the time is right," he had promised, and she had no choice but to be content with that.

Their suite had felt empty on this last, sad night, and she had been lonely so here she was. Now, looking at her handsome "swan" Mark, she was glad she had come.

As the guests arrived, Margo assumed the role of beneficent mistress, warmly greeting the nervous newcomers and helping them settle in for the show. When she and Robert cut their respective submissives, she realized she was having fun. This wasn't real, but the theatrics were entertaining, nonetheless.

Both Rhonda and Mark behaved beautifully, allowing themselves to be cut and suckled, to the awe of the onlookers and pretend vampires in the room. And afterwards, when Margo and Mark retired to one of the many bedrooms for a little sexual play, his gratitude had been abundantly clear. He had been delighted at the new turn their relationship had taken, asking no questions but gracefully accepting whatever she offered. She left him asleep, a smile on his innocent face.

"Where you going?" Robert asked, his voice loud against the silence. He was sitting in the large salon reading a book, a drink in his hand. Rhonda, presumably asleep in his bed, was nowhere to be seen. Margo had assumed everyone would have left or been asleep by now. She startled at the sound of Robert's voice. Please, God, don't let him have any lingering expectations from their one brief encounter, she prayed.

It was now well past midnight and Margo was reasonably sure that Julian and Grace would have returned from their final hunt. She wanted to see them off before they left. Not that she would tell Robert where she was going! She sensed he wasn't to be trusted. He'd made his distaste for Julian clear many times since Julian had "stolen" Grace from the coven.

"Why, home, silly." She kept her voice consciously light. "It's almost daylight. Aren't you exhausted?"

"I'm tired, yes. It was a good night. The fledglings were suitably impressed. Why don't you stay? You and Mark obviously finally did 'the dirty deed'. Seems like you're willing to share it with just about anyone now, eh? Why not me? Why not me again, eh, Margo?"

She bit the retort that rose to her tongue and instead said, "Robert, cher. You're so tired, and I think a little drunk. So I will forgive you, and assume that you don't even realize how rude you're being. Not to mention your lover is asleep at the moment in your bed! Let a lady go home when she's ready, eh?"

Robert glanced toward his bedroom and reason seemed to prevail. He stood and walked with her to the front door. "Don't be such a stranger, Margo. We miss you."

"Yes, yes, I won't," she promised, not knowing if she'd have the heart to return here once her vampires had left her. Walking down the walk, she hurried toward her parked car. Sighing with relief that Robert hadn't tried to "put the moves on her", she sped away toward Julian's hotel.

She didn't notice Robert slipping into his car, silently following her into the heart of the city.

* * * * *

Julian, Grace and Margo exchanged kisses and promises, and some tears as they said goodbye. Dawn was sneaking over the windowsill, and a limousine was waiting below to take the two vampires out of Margo's life.

When the three of them stepped out into the hotel lobby to check out, they saw, of all people, Robert Dalton. He jumped up, shouting, "I knew it! I fucking knew it! You! The mystery European who thinks he can just swoop into my town and take my women!"

He was holding a whiskey and soda, his third. By the time, he'd gotten his car parked, Margo had disappeared somewhere inside the hotel so Robert had determined to wait. She had to come out sometime. He somehow knew she wasn't going home! She was going to fuck that bastard Gaston! First Mark, now this ass! When she could have had him! It was too much.

Now, obviously drunk, he was speaking too loudly for the near-empty lobby, waving his glass for emphasis.

"Control yourself, sir," Julian said, but Robert's face was suddenly reddening, his eyes popping from their sockets with rage.

Robert lurched toward Grace, reaching out to touch her necklace, but she stepped back, gasping. "My amphora! My fucking amphora!" Whirling toward Margo, he yelled, "You bitch! You whore! You used me to get that so you could give it to these—to these," he hesitated and then shouted, "vampires!" Grace clutched the little vial at her throat as people turned to look at what was becoming a scene.

Julian's smooth low voice interrupted, "But aren't you yourself a vampire, Mr. Dalton? Or so you told me when you had us to dinner. A sanguine vampire, I believe you said, sir." Julian's expression was entirely without guile.

"Fuck you. I think you're way more into this stuff than is natural, you know what I'm saying?" Turning to Grace, perhaps an easier target, he spat, "I watched you, Grace, sucking on my swan like there was no tomorrow! You made her sick, did you know that! Weak, she was, for several days after. And you—" he flashed back toward Julian, "—the both of you, so pale with your weird sparkling eyes. Something isn't right here. I suspected it before but I was too much the gentleman to probe! And now you're stealing Margo! Kidnapping her, no doubt! I run this town! The Red Covenant is mine and it's the most influential vampire club in the south! You're messing on my turf, mister!"

Margo touched his arm but Robert pulled away. "Cher, Robert, hush now, you're being ridiculous. You've had too much whiskey."

Julian took the younger man's arm. He was clearly drunk and very angry. Just on the edge of leaving this city, the last thing Julian wanted was a fight with a drunken human. "Let's go back to the suite for a moment, shall we?" Taking Robert's elbow firmly in his grip, he steered him toward the elevator bank.

Surprisingly, Robert went along rather docilely, though he weaved slightly. None of them spoke as the large, elegant elevator sped silently up to the penthouse suite. Even Robert, for all his professed wealth, seemed impressed with the grandeur of the place as they entered. Julian led him to a chair and they all took seats around him.

"Listen, Robert. You're a discerning man. You're observant and obviously intelligent. Our stay in your fair city has come to an end. I am returning to France with Grace. We'll be out of your hair and off your 'turf' by the morning. I'm sorry if we've upset you. No one's being kidnapped. Margo simply came to see us off, to wish us farewell." Margo nodded, as Robert glanced at her. "Margo gave this amphora to Grace as a gift because Grace admired it so.

"It was an amazing act of kindness and a show of your obvious love for Margo that you in turn gave her such a treasure. Your obvious respect and love for her are clear." Julian paused a second as Margo's mind suddenly opened to him and he read in it what she had done to procure this little item, and why. Keeping his features smooth he continued to back Robert into a corner.

"Of course, as you mentioned, you are a gentleman, and gentlemen don't question what ladies do with the gifts they are given. I do hope we are all of an understanding here? Did you need a ride home or would you perhaps like to stay in the suite for a while and recover yourself? We are checking out, but the room is good until 11:00 this morning. You are welcome to stay and rest a bit. You'll find some fine champagne in the refrigerator there under the bar. Please help yourself to it."

"Oh, no, you don't," Robert interjected. "You can't silence me with your fancy words or buy me off. I don't need your stupid suite. I have my own mansion for God's sake!" He took another healthy swig of his drink.

"Just what is it you want, Robert?" Grace spoke for the first time.

He turned toward her, his eyes wild. "I want you to admit what you are. You know as well as I that our clubs and covens are just for kicks. You don't think I honestly believe I'm a vampire. Shit, you mocked me that first time I met you at the Coven Ball. But you!" His glare moved from Grace to Julian. "The two of *you* are something else again. Just admit it to me. Admit what you are. I've been watching the news—all those bums lying around with little holes in their necks. I've been developing my own theories since the two of you showed up." His eyes glittered with mean intelligence.

Julian entered his mind, feeling the confusion that whiskey wrought, but beneath it cruel intentions. Robert planned to expose them, to tell the authorities that these were dangerous people who sucked the blood of others and left them for dead. He didn't honestly believe they were vampires—there was no such thing, of course. But they were dangerous sickos who deserved whatever they got, once he handed them over to the police.

Julian sighed. He had hoped to avoid something like this, but Robert had offered them no choice. As Robert blustered, Julian silently stood and walked around behind him. With a deft movement, he locked his arm around the young man's throat, getting him in a chokehold that soon left him unconscious.

"Oh, God," Margo whispered, "Are you going to kill him?"

"I think we have to," Julian answered. "The poor idiot gives us no choice."

"Please, Julian. Let's just leave him weakened. Leave him so he won't be able to take action until we're long gone. Margo's still got to live here, you know. She doesn't need to be part of a murder investigation."

Julian sighed, letting the two women persuade him. He hoped it wasn't a decision he would come to regret. "Okay, let's take him down the private penthouse elevator to the garages. We'll deposit him near his home and let him come to on his own accord. We'll be gone before he revives. But first, we need to take his blood. To make sure he stays weak and unconscious until we're well away from this cursed place."

Turning toward Grace, he said, "Would you like the honors, my greedy girl?"

"Oh, Julian, no. No, I would rather you did it. Somehow I haven't the appetite at the moment." Julian knelt behind Robert, who just looked now as if he were sleeping, all the wrinkles of rage smoothed from his face. As Margo watched, her expression one of mixed horror and fascination, Julian bit down, his canines distending into sharp little points that pierced Robert's flesh with ease. He sucked deeply, drawing the man's blood until Robert was pale, his head fallen limp against his chest.

Grace lightly touched Julian's shoulder and he shuddered, but slowly released his grip. A droplet of blood remained at Robert's throat and Julian leaned back down, licking it away with a flick of his tongue. Turning to Margo, he said, "You've seen something no human should see. But this is an unusual situation and I don't want to risk the safety of either one of you. Hopefully he won't remember the events just preceding this, or the taking of the blood here. Luckily for us vampires, humans seem to have no memory for these things. I don't want him making life difficult for you, Margo."

"Don't worry, cher, I've taken care of myself all these years. Robert is easy to handle, don't you worry. I'll have him talking to himself by the time I'm done with him. Vampire? There's no such thing as vampires, you silly boy!" she grinned.

He stood still a moment, and then laughed a hollow little laugh. "To think — I've been alone for so long and suddenly two lovely women are by my side, with all my secrets at their disposal."

"Perhaps we are your new circle, Julian. A circle of three?" Margo said hopefully. She still hadn't entirely put her dream of being "turned" to rest.

Julian was aware of the subtext of her words. He looked sharply at Margo, sensing her unspoken but still intent longing to go with them, and to be turned. He'd learned after many years that it was better to let things flow than to try and control them. It seemed that Margo had dropped into his life just as surely as Grace had. He would wait and see what her path was to be and how it would cross his and Grace's as they set out on this new part of the journey.

Now he only said, "Come on, let's unload this stupid boy. Grace and I have a plane to catch!

Epilogue

The sky was a brilliant dark blue, fading into a twilight of color that made Grace catch her breath. "We call it *le bleu* in French literature," Julian offered. His arm was loosely draped over her shoulder as they stood on the crest of a low hill overlooking the fields of his native lands in the Champagne region of France. "Somehow the twilight is more brilliant here in France than anywhere else on earth."

"It's lovely," she breathed. The sun was setting fast over the low, smooth hills at the horizon. Their flight had been uneventful and Grace had been so focused on making an escape and then settling down in their hotel in Paris that she'd barely had time to take in the fact that she was actually on French soil.

They had each hunted the second evening in Paris. For Grace, it was her first time out alone and she felt empowered by her ability to stalk, subdue and take her feed without being observed and without harming her prey. How she loved the silky, pure power the blood gave her. It spread through her limbs like hot wine, but unlike liquor, it left her head clear, her thoughts focused, her body buoyant and strong.

After a lifetime of feeling enfeebled and not at home in her own skin, what an experience now! To be free and alive, with the knowledge that she had all the time in the world to hone her skills and share the love she had found with this amazing man.

They had taken the scenic drive out to what used to be his father's properties so long ago. As the sky darkened to a purple gray, Julian bent his head toward his lover and kissed her. A warm summer breeze wafted gently, lifting the tendrils of silky hair that framed her face.

Without speaking they sank together on the soft heather, their lips still locked in a kiss. Julian reached down, easing open the little buttons that held Grace's long flowing summer dress closed. Pulling back from her a little, he swooped down his head toward her. She was naked beneath the open dress — save for little panties that barely concealed her auburn pubic curls. She sighed with pleasure as Julian suckled and licked at her sensitive nipples.

Reaching blindly, she opened Julian's soft cotton shirt, pulling it back to reveal his firm smooth chest. She trailed a hand down his body, her nails lightly grazing his skin until her fingers met the buttons of his faded denim jeans. With a pull, she opened the fly, her hands greedily seeking his hard cock.

As Julian sat back, she leaned forward. Lovingly she took his member into her mouth, savoring its pungent sweetness as she licked and caressed it with her tongue and hands. Julian groaned with pleasure and whispered, "I adore you, beautiful girl."

Grace tickled and teased Julian's balls and cock until he was panting with desire. "Stop," he managed to gasp. "I want to see you. Stand up, my sweet, submissive girl. Take off those panties." Obediently, Grace released his cock from her passionate grip and stood in a graceful lithe movement, dropping her silky panties to the ground.

She was no longer the skinny, lonely paralegal from a small Louisiana town, wondering when her pain would stop and her life would begin. She felt like some kind of vampire princess in a perfect fairytale. And Julian was her lord prince — truly the man of her dreams. For hadn't she dreamed of just this moment, over and over again, in her little apartment on many a hot summer's night in sultry old New Orleans? Yes, Julian had been the man in the dreams and now he stood before her, his large dark eyes focused solely on her.

Grace didn't feel awkward standing naked for her lover. She felt at peace and eager for his touch, desperate for it, her sex hot and wet with need. Her long, pale body gleamed in the last light of the setting sun. Julian, standing now naked as well, pressed his strong, hard body against hers.

"I want your blood, Grace. I want to claim you in every way."

"And I you, my lord," she whispered, letting her head fall back so that her long hair streamed out behind her.

Tenderly they bit, each gently sucking at the soft flesh where neck met shoulder. Their bodies pressed close, her nipples tingling against his chest as they sank together again in the soft grasses. Hot, sweet blood coursed between them as they held one another. When Julian entered her, Grace gave a cry of animal pleasure, shuddering and jerking against him in almost immediate orgasm.

Together they rocked and moved, their mouths still suckling, drinking the powerful elixir of the blood of the true kin as they fucked with deliberate slowness. There was no hurry. Life had taken on a different pace now, and one night was nothing but a moment in time. The minutes slipped into hours as they made love, their bodies connected through sex and blood, through delicious heat and stinging pain, weaving together in a perfect sacred circle that seemed to have no beginning and no end. The moon had risen high in the sky and was slipping down the other side of its night arc when Julian uttered a little cry and arched hard against his lover, shuddering his pleasure into her.

They lay still for some moments, or was it hours? The wind blew gently, finally chilling Grace who shivered and opened her eyes, looking up at the moon. It was so bright it partially obscured the myriad of tiny stars glimmering in its wake.

"Why, Julian," she remarked. "I do believe that's the second full moon this month."

"Yes," he answered, staring up at the sky. "A blue moon."

Enjoy this excerpt from
Turning Tricks
© Copyright Claire Thompson, 2005

All Rights Reserved, Ellora's Cave Publishing, Inc.

Turning Tricks

Smiling a little nervously she said, "Andrew. Please kiss me."

He put his things on the little table next to the chair and said, "Excuse me?"

She closed her eyes and whispered throatily, "Please. I want you to kiss me. Like you did in the restaurant. Please." Her heart was already pounding and she knew if he rejected her now she would die.

He didn't need to be asked again. Andrew stood and took Ashley's hands in his. Pulling her up, he took her in his arms and leaned over her, slowly touching her lips with his. After a moment his tongue found hers and his arms enfolded her body, pulling her up hard against him. His kiss was sweet but ardent. She could feel his desire, his longing and she rose up to meet it with equal intensity.

She could feel his erection rise through his jeans. She loved the feel of him, the taste of him, the smell of him. This was so different from the gropings she "allowed" her johns—though she hated when they tried to kiss her and they rarely tried. Instead of feeling stiff and empty in their arms, now Ashley felt as if her nerve endings were electrified. Every touch of his mouth or his hands sent shivers of pleasure ripping through her.

"Andrew, Andrew," she murmured between kisses. She felt almost faint with need. A pulsing deep in her sex made her feel wanton and womanly. It was all so new. It was at once frightening and alluring. She pulled away and Andrew let her go.

"Can we go to the bedroom?" she whispered, pressing her face against his chest.

"Ashley, I'm not sure it's a good idea."

She felt the heat in her face as shame flooded her. Her fledgling self-confidence seemed to evaporate in the face of his rejection. So, he *didn't* want her. It had been a "mercy" kiss because he felt sorry for the poor little waif girl he'd plucked from the shelter.

When it came down to it, why would he want to lie with a whore? With a slut that had been fucked by countless faceless men. The fact that she'd hated every second of it didn't matter. Without realizing she was doing it, Ashley's fist punched into Andrew's chest, hard.

"Hey! What's this about?" He grabbed her wrist in a firm grip and a weird sort of thrill zinged through her. His grip was hard. He didn't hurt her but she could feel his strength. Even so, she wasn't afraid, her hurt feelings overriding any fear. She balled up the other fist and punched him again. As she had secretly wanted him to, Andrew grabbed that wrist as well. She stared up at him, her eyes blazing, trembling with a mixture of anger, humiliation and still fierce desire.

Her anger was blended with this new strange excitement at being held captive in Andrew's strong grip. She didn't understand the feeling but her body responded as her nipples pressed against the thin fabric of the T-shirt.

"'Cause you don't want me, you bastard! 'Cause you liked me when you thought I was a bored housewife. Maybe I was off-limits then and so you were allowed to want me from afar, but now that you know I'm just a whore you don't want me!"

Andrew dropped her wrists and stood back, his face a study in compassion and disbelief. "Ashley," he said in a whisper. "You are so wrong, you sweet, silly girl. How could you possibly think that? Do you have *any idea* the willpower I've exerted to keep from jumping your bones every minute of every day since you've been here? Jesus Christ, Ashley, with you parading around in that old shirt with no bra, your gorgeous breasts outlined so sweetly. Those legs that won't end in my old gym shorts. The way your hair falls like a golden storm over the pillow when you're sleeping..." his voice cracked, and now it was Andrew who fell to his kneels, wrapping his arms around Ashley's waist.

Burying his head against her thigh he murmured, "Ashley, darling. Not *want* you? Oh, my love, there is *nothing* I want more than you. But I don't want to push you! To rush you. To take what I want out of greed because you're vulnerable and needy. Because you might feel beholden to me. Because your whole life has been one man after another taking and taking and taking from you with no thought to your needs, to what *you* want.

"No. I never want to be like that with you. I want whatever you want to give me, offered freely. I will never abuse your trust. Never, I promise you."

Tears sprang to Ashley's eyes at Andrew's sweet speech. She smoothed his dark head, dumfounded. This was even better than the romance novels, because this was *real*.

About the Author

Claire Thompson has written numerous novels and short stories, all exploring aspects of Dominance & submission. Ms. Thompson's gentler novels seek not only to tell a story, but to come to grips with, and ultimately exalt in the true beauty and spirituality of a loving exchange of power. Her darker works press the envelope of what is erotic and what can be a sometimes dangerous slide into the world of sadomasochism. She writes about the timeless themes of sexuality and romance, with twists and curves to examine the 'darker' side of the human psyche. Ultimately Claire's work deals with the human condition, and our constant search for love and intensity of experience.

Claire welcomes mail from readers. You can write to her c/o Ellora's Cave Publishing at 1056 Home Avenue, Akron OH 44310-3502.

Why an electronic book?

We live in the Information Age—an exciting time in the history of human civilization in which technology rules supreme and continues to progress in leaps and bounds every minute of every hour of every day. For a multitude of reasons, more and more avid literary fans are opting to purchase e-books instead of paperbacks. The question to those not yet initiated to the world of electronic reading is simply: *why?*

1. *Price.* An electronic title at Ellora's Cave Publishing and Cerridwen Press runs anywhere from 40-75% less than the cover price of the <u>exact same title</u> in paperback format. Why? Cold mathematics. It is less expensive to publish an e-book than it is to publish a paperback, so the savings are passed along to the consumer.

2. *Space.* Running out of room to house your paperback books? That is one worry you will never have with electronic novels. For a low one-time cost, you can purchase a handheld computer designed specifically for e-reading purposes. Many e-readers are larger than the average handheld, giving you plenty of screen room. Better yet, hundreds of titles can be stored within your new library—a single microchip. (Please note that Ellora's Cave and Cerridwen Press does not endorse any specific brands. You can check our website at www.ellorascave.com or

www.cerridwenpress.com for customer recommendations we make available to new consumers.)

3. *Mobility*. Because your new library now consists of only a microchip, your entire cache of books can be taken with you wherever you go.

4. *Personal preferences are accounted for*. Are the words you are currently reading too small? Too large? Too...**ANNOYING**? Paperback books cannot be modified according to personal preferences, but e-books can.

5. *Instant gratification*. Is it the middle of the night and all the bookstores are closed? Are you tired of waiting days—sometimes weeks—for online and offline bookstores to ship the novels you bought? Ellora's Cave Publishing sells instantaneous downloads 24 hours a day, 7 days a week, 365 days a year. Our e-book delivery system is 100% automated, meaning your order is filled as soon as you pay for it.

Those are a few of the top reasons why electronic novels are displacing paperbacks for many an avid reader. As always, Ellora's Cave and Cerridwen Press welcomes your questions and comments. We invite you to email us at service@ellorascave.com, service@cerridwenpress.com or write to us directly at: 1056 Home Ave. Akron OH 44310-3502.

Ellora's Cavemen

Legendary Tails

Try an e-book for your immediate
reading pleasure or order these titles in print from

www.EllorasCave.com

Ellora's Cave
The Best in Today's Romantica™

THE
✟ ELLORA'S CAVE ✟
LIBRARY

Stay up to date with Ellora's Cave Titles in
Print with our Quarterly Catalog.

To recieve a catalog,
send an email with your name
and mailing address to:

CATALOG@ELLORASCAVE.COM

or send a letter or postcard
with your mailing address to:

Catalog Request
c/o Ellora's Cave Publishing, Inc.
1056 Home Avenue
Akron, Ohio 44310-3502

erridwen, the Celtic Goddess of wisdom, was the muse who brought inspiration to storytellers and those in the creative arts. Cerridwen Press encompasses the best and most innovative stories in all genres of today's fiction. Visit our site and discover the newest titles by talented authors who still get inspired - much like the ancient storytellers did, once upon a time.

CERRIDWEN PRESS

www.cerridwenpress.com

Discover for yourself why readers can't get enough of
the multiple award-winning publisher
Ellora's Cave.
Whether you prefer e-books or paperbacks,
be sure to visit EC on the web at
www.ellorascave.com
for an erotic reading experience that will leave you
breathless.